Mt. Sterling Public Library
60 W. Columbus St.
Mt. Sterling, Ohio 43143

Librarians Book Express
9/07 22.95   69839

# DIABETES

# DIABETES

**MARLENE TARG BRILL**

Twenty-First Century Medical Library

 Twenty-First Century Books
Minneapolis

*Many people helped the author gather information and prepare this book. She wishes to thank the following people for their assistance: Marlene Davis, LCSW, clinical social worker specializing in chronic diseases; Dr. Ellen Rosenberg, psychologist; Christine Taylor, permissions, American Diabetes Association; Dr. William Thomas, pathologist; Dr. Amy Criego, pediatric endocrinologist, Park Nicollet Clinic; Dr. Meryl Abensohn; Michael Glazer; Sidney Medintz; Lauren Rosenberg; Doug Rosenberg; and Ralph von dem Hagen. A special thank-you goes to all the caring families who shared their stories so others can understand and help prevent diabetes.*

Copyright © 2008 by Marlene Targ Brill

All rights reserved. International copyright secured. No part of this book may be reproduced, stored in a retrieval system, or transmitted in any form or by any means— electronic, mechanical, photocopying, recording, or otherwise— without the prior written permission of Lerner Publishing Group, Inc., except for the inclusion of brief quotations in an acknowledged review.

Twenty-First Century Books
A division of Lerner Publishing Group, Inc.
241 First Avenue North
Minneapolis, MN 55401 U.S.A.

Website address: www.lernerbooks.com

Library of Congress Cataloging-in-Publication Data

Brill, Marlene Targ.
   Diabetes / by Marlene Targ Brill.
     p. cm. — (Twenty-first medical library)
   Includes bibliographical references and index.
   ISBN 978-0-8225-6785-1 (lib. bdg. : alk. paper)
    1. Diabetes—Juvenile literature. 2. Diabetes—Case studies—Juvenile literature.  I. Title.
RC660.5.B75 2008
616.4'62—dc22                                                                                   2006101392

Manufactured in the United States of America
1 2 3 4 5 6 – BP – 13 12 11 10 09 08

# Contents

*Chapter 1*
**THE SUGAR DISEASE**
7

*Chapter 2*
**TYPES OF DIABETES**
18

*Chapter 3*
**DETECTING DIABETES**
29

*Chapter 4*
**TAKING CONTROL**
37

*Chapter 5*
**MEDICATIONS AND INSULIN**
56

*Chapter 6*
**PROBLEMS OF UNCONTROLLED DIABETES**
64

*Chapter 7*
**ADJUSTING TO LIFE WITH DIABETES**
75

*Chapter 8*
**DARK HISTORY, BRIGHTER FUTURE**
90

**GLOSSARY**
100

**RESOURCES**
106

**SOURCES**
110

**SELECTED BIBLIOGRAPHY**
112

**INDEX**
114

Chapter 1

# THE SUGAR DISEASE

## Jared's Story

*When Jared was in seventh grade, his mother noticed that he often became extremely hungry and thirsty, which made him urinate more. Yet even though Jared ate more than ever, he was losing weight and felt tired. Since Jared never complained of feeling sick, his mother thought this was normal for an athletic thirteen-year-old.*

*During a routine physical exam, Jared's doctor asked him to leave a urine sample. Later, Jared's mother received a call from the doctor's office requesting that Jared come back for a blood test the next morning before eating. The test showed high levels of sugar in Jared's blood. The doctor said he has* diabetes. *Jared and his mother were shocked.*

## UNDERSTANDING DIABETES

A diagnosis of diabetes can be overwhelming. Families wonder what diabetes is and what the disease means for the person who has it. Finding answers to these questions is the first step to understanding and managing diabetes.

Diabetes occurs when the body cannot use sugar properly. The disease is marked by high levels of *blood sugar*, or *glucose*. Glucose enters the bloodstream from food you eat and drink and provides energy the body needs to carry out daily activities. Diabetes interferes with the way the body makes or uses *insulin*, a chemical produced by the *pancreas*, a small organ that lies behind the lower part of the stomach.

In healthy individuals, insulin allows glucose to move from blood into the body's cells. Inside the cells, glucose is converted into energy. When cells cannot absorb glucose, sugar collects in the bloodstream or leaves the body in urine. Without sugar the body loses energy, resulting in a host of different symptoms.

Records dating as far back as 1500 B.C. describe symptoms of diabetes. Ancient Egyptian medical papers refer to a disease in which people "cannot stop either... drinking or making water." In the second century A.D., the Greek doctor Aretaeus noted that in some patients, "flesh and limbs melt into urine." Aretaeus named the condition "diabetes," from the Greek word for siphon. The term referred to the way diabetes draws water from the body, similar to liquid moving through a siphon.

In a 1674 medical book on diabetes, English doctor Thomas Willis reported that his patients' urine "was wonderfully sweet as if it were imbued with Honey or Sugar." Scientists debated the idea of sweet urine and its origins until 1776, when another British doctor, Matthew Dobson, conducted an experiment. Dobson

Thomas Willis (1621–1675) was an English physician. At one time, diabetes was called Willis's disease.

collected 2 quarts (1.9 liters) of urine from a patient who complained of excessive thirst, frequent urinating, weakness, and cracked skin. Dobson heated the urine sample until all the liquid evaporated, leaving a layer of white, sweet-smelling granules. In a bold move, he tasted the substance and confirmed that it was sugar.

Dobson reasoned that the sugar could not have formed in the kidneys, as earlier doctors had proposed. The kidneys filter waste products from the blood and release the body's waste and excess water as urine. Instead, Dobson argued that sugar in urine originated in the blood. Scientists still had no idea how sugar got into the bloodstream or what to do about it. But Dobson's declaration linked diabetes to sugar in urine and blood. Later doctors added the Latin term *mellitus*, or "honey sweet," to the term *diabetes* to describe the sweet taste.

## GLUCOSE AND INSULIN

Glucose is important because it serves as the body's main source of fuel for growth and activity. Glucose from food is converted into energy during the process of *digestion*. When you eat, your digestive organs release chemicals that break down food into smaller, usable particles. The particles—including glucose—go to different parts of the body to help them function. Glucose enters the bloodstream and travels throughout the body, nourishing individual cells in muscles and tissues.

For cells to accept glucose, however, they must receive signals from *hormones* that aid digestion. Hormones are chemical messengers that travel in body fluids and stimulate cells to do their job. Hormones control many body processes, such as growth; sexual functions; and *metabolism*, the way the body chemically changes food into nutrients for growth and energy. Glands and organs that produce hormones make up the *endocrine system*. These glands and organs secrete, or release, hormones that go directly into the bloodstream. Most hormones circulate throughout the body, but each hormone affects only a limited number of cells.

The hormone insulin allows cells to receive glucose. Insulin is produced in the pancreas by clusters of cells called *islets*, or islets of Langerhans. Within the islets, *beta cells* manufacture insulin. Insulin acts as the gatekeeper that allows sugar into cells. The hormone helps regulate glucose levels in the bloodstream so just enough is available to provide cells with fuel for energy. Throughout the day, *blood glucose* levels vary, depending on what you eat and how active you are. Too little glucose leaves the body without the energy it needs.

Other organs and chemicals also play roles in controlling glucose levels. The liver, an organ above the stomach, stores extra sugar for use in between meals and snacks.

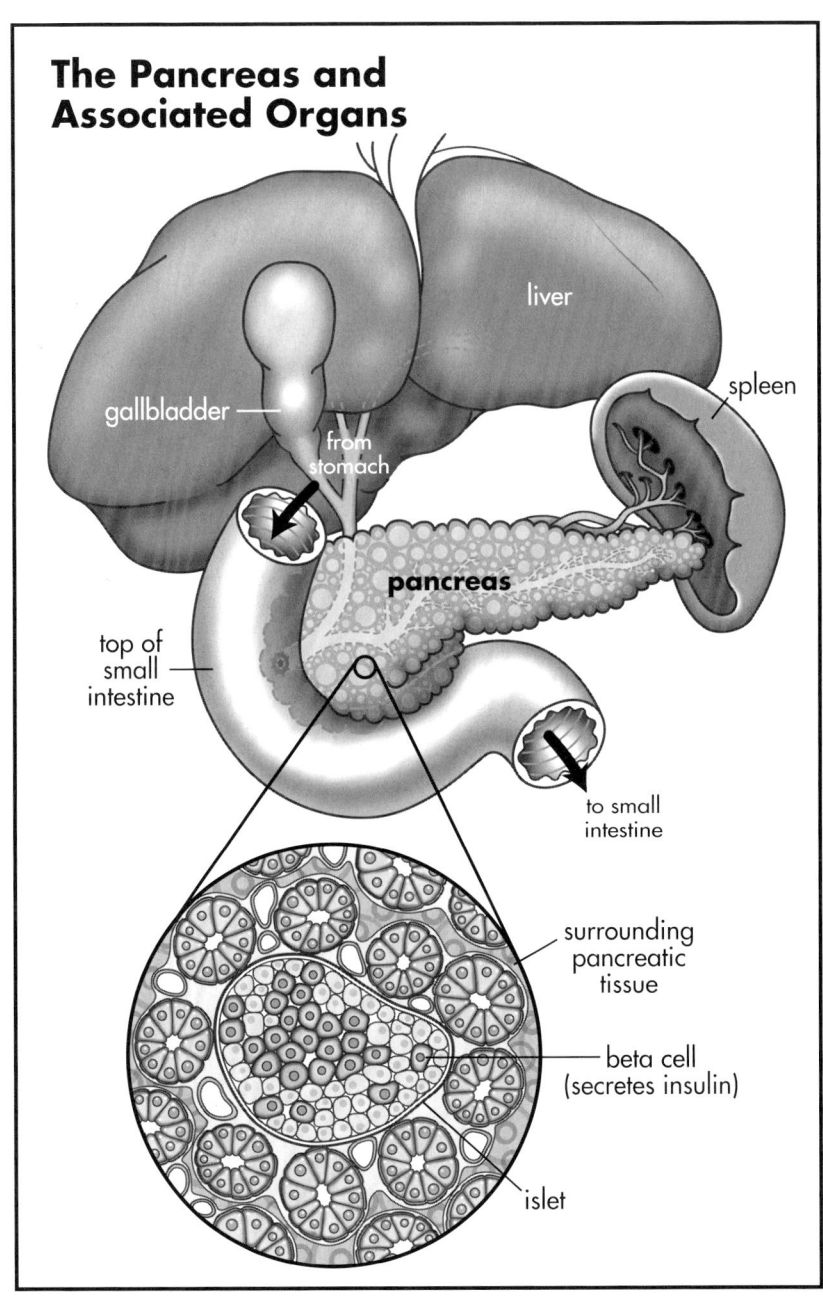

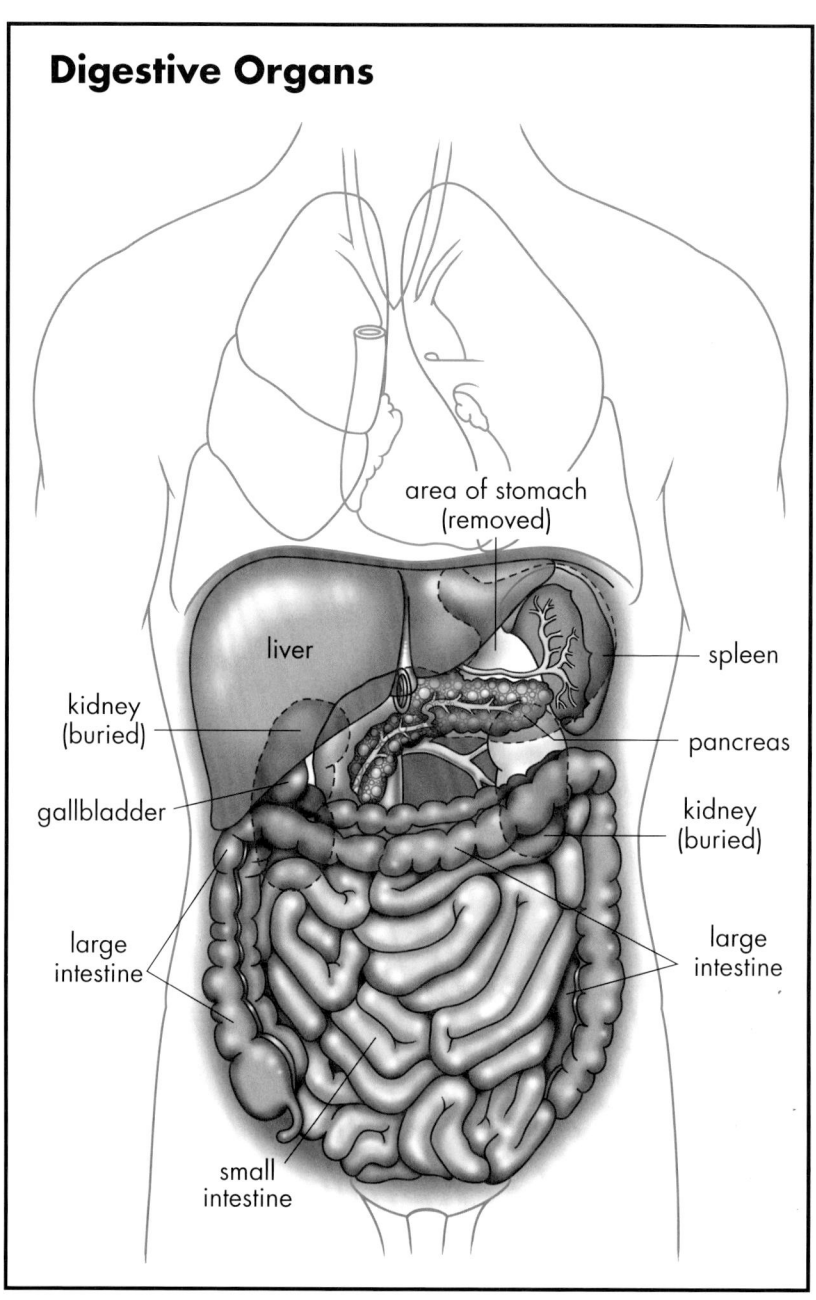

When blood glucose levels drop too low and the body needs energy, the liver converts stored sugar—called *glycogen*—into glucose. The glucose is then released into the bloodstream. This process restores blood sugar levels to a healthy range.

Insulin and other hormones perform a balancing act to regulate blood sugar levels and provide fuel for cells. In healthy people, this process occurs automatically. Blood sugar levels stay within a set range. In people with diabetes, the body either cannot manufacture enough insulin or cannot use it properly. Glucose collects in the bloodstream instead of going into cells. Over time, high levels of blood sugar damage organs and body systems.

## SIGNS AND SYMPTOMS

High levels of sugar in the blood and not enough sugar fueling body cells cause a range of diabetes symptoms. They may appear abruptly or gradually, depending on how well the body produces and uses insulin. Many people, such as Jared, experience no early signs of the disease. Some types of diabetes can go undetected for years.

Other people know quickly that something is wrong. Often the first signs of diabetes are excessive thirst and a need to urinate frequently. "Diabetes is called the drinking and peeing disease," Jared explains.

### Increased Thirst and Urination

Excess sugar draws water from body tissues. The sugary water is excreted, or eliminated, into urine. If urine contains too much sugar, the kidneys flush out extra water to make the urine less sugary. This creates even more urine, prompting extra trips to the bathroom. Excessive urination leads to increased thirst to replenish the body's water supply. The cycle of drinking more liquids and urinating frequently continues.

**Fatigue**
Without proper fuel, the body tires more easily. People with poorly controlled or uncontrolled diabetes often have less energy than others their age. They might feel tired, exhausted, or irritable. They may perspire, tremble, or feel weak and confused. Sometimes diabetes causes symptoms similar to those of the flu.

**Weight Changes and Increased Hunger**
Without life-giving sugar, starved cells search to replace the necessary fuel. The need for fuel leads to increased appetite. Depending on the type of diabetes, some people gain weight from excessive eating to replace nutrients that leave the body, while others eat more food than usual and still lose weight. Without enough glucose for nourishment, their bodies burn fat for energy instead.

Diabetes can make some people lose weight effortlessly. Others gain weight. Neither weight change is healthy.

### Blurred Vision
High blood sugar levels interfere with the balance of fluids in the eyes. Glucose can suck liquid from the eyes' lenses, thinning them and causing problems with focusing. Increased blood sugar over a long period of time may also cause blood vessels in the eyes to bleed. Bleeding or leaking of fluid can damage vessels and cause light flashes, spots, or halos around lights. Blurry vision from thinning lenses improves as blood sugar levels return to normal. But other vision problems require attention from an eye doctor.

### Healing Difficulties
Uncontrolled diabetes impairs the body's ability to battle germs and heal from infections, cuts, and bruises. People with diabetes may face more frequent infections, such as in the bladder or skin. Their gums may become red, swollen, and tender, and they may have other dental and mouth problems.

### Other Signs and Symptoms
Other signs and symptoms of diabetes may include:

- Headache
- Dry, itchy skin
- Tingling feet and hands
- Abdominal pain
- Nausea
- Vomiting

## A GROWING EPIDEMIC

In the last two decades, the number of people with diabetes worldwide has skyrocketed from 30 million to 230 million. The World Health Organization estimates that this number could reach 366 million by 2030. Cases in the United States alone reached almost 21

### WHAT'S IN A NAME?

Many people with diabetes dislike being labeled "diabetic." They believe the term limits who they are and what they can accomplish. A better way to talk about diabetes is to put the person first, by saying "people with diabetes" or "person who has diabetes." The term *diabetic* can be reserved to describe supplies or complications linked to the disease.

million in 2005, double the number from two decades ago. Another 41 million people tested with blood sugar levels high enough to be diagnosed with *prediabetes*, with an increased risk of developing the disease.

Health officials fear that diabetes has become an epidemic. "Diabetes is this massive tidal wave hitting the country," said Dr. Aldo Rossini, director of the Diabetes Division at the University of Miami. The Centers for Disease Control and Prevention (CDC) projects that one in three U.S. children under the age of five will test with high sugar levels sometime during their life span.

This epidemic brings grave consequences. Diabetes is the sixth-deadliest illness in the United States. It can lead to heart disease, kidney disease, blindness, loss of limbs, and other serious problems that disrupt lives and are expensive to treat.

The medical community faces challenges in communicating the message about soaring rates of diabetes and what the diagnosis means. Many people with diabetes do not realize that high blood sugar can harm them, because they feel fine. Without concrete signs, newly diagnosed patients and those with prediabetes do not believe they are really sick. Yet early treatment remains important for preventing further damage. Changes in diet and activity, as well as medications, can help prevent or reduce complications of diabetes.

## LEARNING ABOUT DIABETES

Diabetes is a chronic, or lifelong, disease without a cure. Treatment requires individuals and families to make life-altering changes. A valuable first step toward getting help is to learn how diabetes works, what signs to watch for, and how to keep sugar levels in check.

"You can't depend upon anyone else to find out what's right for your body," says Carl, aged fifty-eight, who has had sugar-related problems since he turned nineteen. "You need to read for yourself or explore on the Internet. Knowledge insures a healthier life."

At a college community health fair in Florida, volunteer representatives of the American Diabetes Association (ADA) display information about diabetes.

*Chapter 2*

# TYPES OF DIABETES

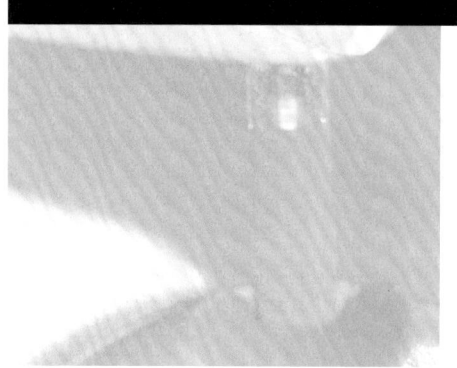

## Shawna's Story

*Eleven-year-old Shawna was thirsty all the time. Because she drank a lot of water and other liquids, she made frequent trips to the bathroom. Just after her twelfth birthday, Shawna's parents took her and a friend to a resort for summer vacation. One day Shawna's friend watched in surprise as Shawna drank five large glasses of iced tea in one hour. Shawna looked weak. She said her eyes felt funny, and her mouth seemed dry. Her friend suggested that maybe Shawna had diabetes.*

*Back home, Shawna's mother took her to the pediatrician, a doctor for children and teens. He tested Shawna's blood and learned that she had type 1 diabetes. Her treatment involved testing her blood throughout the day and watching her diet. Because of the type of diabetes she had, Shawna also needed daily injections of insulin to replace what her body did not produce.*

## Jay's Story

*Jay was a successful computer technician and passionate gamer. He often got so involved in his work and computer games that he took little time to prepare healthy meals. For lunch he grabbed a burger and ate it at his desk, and for supper he frequently picked up pizza on his way home. Because Jay spent most of his time in front of the computer, he rarely exercised. Over the years, he steadily gained weight. By the time he was forty years old, he was obese.*

*Suddenly Jay dropped twenty pounds without trying. He felt thirsty all the time. Yet his eating and exercise habits had not changed. Jay turned to his doctor for answers. She discovered that Jay had* type 2 diabetes. *She prescribed pills to lower his blood sugar. She also referred Jay to a nutritionist, a specialist in managing food choices. The nutritionist helped him learn to control his glucose levels by following a healthy diet and exercising regularly.*

### ONE DISEASE, DIFFERENT TYPES

Problems with blood sugar can develop from a variety of causes. Doctors give diabetes different names based on the specific reason for the disease. The main forms of diabetes—type 1, type 2, and *gestational*—all create blood sugar problems but from different origins.

In the past, type 2 diabetes mainly targeted older, overweight people, while type 1 usually began in the teen years. But doctors observed that older people do develop type 1 diabetes, and the number of younger people with type 2 is increasing.

In the last twenty years, the number of kids with diabetes has increased dramatically. Children spend less time in physical activities, such as sports, recess, and outdoor play and more time watching television, playing video games, and messaging or working on computers. Typical diets include soda pop, chips, candy, and other sugary and high-fat foods. Lack of physical activity and eating too many unhealthy foods can lead to obesity, which contributes to type 2 diabetes. According to the Centers for Disease Control and Prevention, one in three children born in the United States in 2000 will likely develop type 2 diabetes unless they get more exercise and improve their diet.

## TYPE 1 DIABETES

In type 1 diabetes, the pancreas produces little or no insulin. Without this crucial hormone, sugar stays in the bloodstream and cannot be used to fuel body cells. People with type 1 diabetes take insulin daily to ensure that sugar can enter their cells.

About 5 percent to 10 percent of all people with diabetes have type 1. The disease generally begins in childhood or the teen years, although anyone can develop type 1 diabetes at any time. Type 1 used to be called juvenile-onset diabetes, or insulin-dependent diabetes.

With type 1 diabetes, the body's *immune system* attacks and destroys beta cells in the pancreas. A healthy immune system protects the body from disease and infection. When a foreign organism, such as bacteria or a virus, enters the body, the immune system sends out an army of cells to flag and destroy the invader. Immune system proteins called *antibodies* help cells recognize and remember the foreign substance. Long-term cell memory fortifies the body against future invasion by the same organism.

Sometimes the immune system produces a type of antibody called *autoantibodies*. Autoantibodies cannot distinguish between an intruder and the body's own cells. Autoantibodies mistakenly attack healthy cells. They may destroy tissues and organs, causing a variety of diseases known as *autoimmune diseases*. Type 1 diabetes is an autoimmune disease in which the immune system attacks beta cells that produce insulin.

Scientists do not know exactly why the body's immune system attacks itself. Many researchers believe that some people inherit a predisposition, or tendency, to develop type 1 diabetes. Then something in the environment, such as a virus, triggers the disease. Illness places stress on the body, requiring more fuel in the cells for energy. The pancreas rushes to produce more insulin to meet the demand. As demand for insulin increases, the body makes autoantibodies that destroy the beta cells. Over time autoantibodies destroy more beta cells. When most of the beta cells are gone, symptoms of diabetes appear.

In a small number of cases, type 1 diabetes does not stem from an immune system problem. Researchers aren't sure what causes this form of the disease, but it tends to be inherited. Most people with this rare type 1 diabetes are of African, Hispanic, or Asian origin. Their treatment may involve fewer doses of insulin.

## TYPE 2 DIABETES

Type 2 is the most common form of diabetes, accounting for 90 to 95 percent of cases. Type 2 diabetes is not an autoimmune disease. With type 2 diabetes, the pancreas usually continues to produce insulin. But for unknown reasons, beta cells do not make enough insulin, or the body's muscle and fat cells no longer recognize insulin, or both to some degree. Rejection of insulin is known as *insulin resistance*. When sugar cannot enter the cells, it remains in the bloodstream, building to dangerous amounts.

While symptoms of type 1 diabetes usually appear abruptly, type 2 symptoms may emerge slowly. Insulin production gradually decreases and resistance increases. Type 2 diabetes can go undetected for years.

Scientists are unsure why cells resist insulin. They do know that excess weight and body fat contribute to developing type 2 diabetes. Being overweight forces the pancreas to work harder to manufacture extra insulin to balance sugar going into the cells. As the demand for insulin rises, the pancreas loses its ability to produce enough. People who are overweight are more likely to have insulin resistance because fat interferes with the body's ability to use insulin.

Obesity is not the only cause of type 2 diabetes. About 10 percent of people with type 2 are not over-

## TYPE 1 AND TYPE 2 DIABETES

|  | Usual Ages | Symptoms | Cause | Treatment |
|---|---|---|---|---|
| **Type 1** | Children/ teens | Appears suddenly | No or little insulin production | Insulin |
| **Type 2** | Adults/ some kids | Develops over years | Not enough insulin; cells resist insulin | Exercise, diet, pills, insulin |

weight. Scientists are investigating the role of family history and environmental factors in development of type 2 diabetes.

In the past, type 2 diabetes was known as adult-onset diabetes because it typically occurred among middle-age or older adults. Over the last two decades, however, greater numbers of children and adolescents have developed the disease. Doctors link this trend to the decrease in physical activity and increase in obesity.

Many people of all ages with type 2 diabetes find they can control sugar levels by exercising more, eating better, and losing weight. They may also need diabetes medication or insulin injections to manage their glucose levels.

## GESTATIONAL DIABETES

Gestational diabetes develops during pregnancy. About 3 to 8 percent of pregnant women develop this form of diabetes, most often in the later months of pregnancy. Changing hormone levels in pregnancy can trigger increased insulin resistance. Hormones produced by the placenta, the organ carrying the unborn baby, cause the mother's body cells to resist insulin. As the placenta grows, it releases more hormones. In some women, the pancreas cannot meet the added demand for insulin. The result is a condition similar to type 2 diabetes.

Often a woman with gestational diabetes experiences no obvious symptoms. Doctors usually screen pregnant women for the disease. If a woman tests positive for gestational diabetes, her doctor usually recommends a special diet. If dietary changes fail to control sugar levels, the woman may receive training about how to check her blood glucose levels and inject insulin.

At the same time, doctors monitor a woman's weight and the baby's movements to ensure a healthy delivery and baby. Babies tend to grow larger in women

Gestational diabetes usually goes away after the baby is born.

who have uncontrolled diabetes. This can be dangerous for both the mother and baby.

Gestational diabetes usually disappears after the baby is born. Hormones given off by the placenta drop to pre-pregnancy levels. But women with gestational diabetes have a one in three chance of developing type 2 diabetes later.

## OTHER TYPES OF DIABETES

Between 1 and 5 percent of diabetes cases do not fall into common diabetes categories. One rare form of diabetes is maturity-onset diabetes of the young (MODY). This inherited condition affects children and teens and causes problems with producing enough insulin. Many people with this disease are a normal weight, and they often can control their blood sugar levels with diet and exercise.

# RISK FACTORS

Unlike the flu or colds, diabetes cannot spread from one person to another. But certain factors increase the risk of developing diabetes, particularly type 2. Some risk factors, such as aging or ethnic background, cannot be avoided. But other factors involve lifestyle choices that can be controlled. These include lack of physical activity and excess weight.

## Family History

A key factor in developing diabetes is family history. People whose family members have type 1 or type 2 diabetes are more likely to develop the disease themselves. If a parent, brother, or sister has type 1 diabetes, a person's risk is fifteen times greater than for someone without a family history of type 1 diabetes. The link between family history and type 2 diabetes is strong but less clear cut.

Scientists are exploring whether a defect in one or more *genes* contributes to diabetes. Genes are basic units of heredity, the passing of traits from parent to offspring. Every human body contains trillions of cells. Each cell includes a set of rod-shaped *chromosomes*, which hold many genes. Genes carry instructions for making proteins that perform most life functions and ensure that the body grows, develops, and works properly. Genes determine physical characteristics, such as hair color, height, and voice quality, and other traits.

Researchers have discovered several genes that may work together to increase a person's odds of developing type 1 diabetes. One set of genes targets specific antibodies and directs them to destroy healthy cells in the pancreas. Under certain conditions, genetic defects may lead to type 1 diabetes.

Scientists believe that genes contribute to the onset of type 2 diabetes as well. They have uncovered a protein that prevents cells from receiving insulin.

Professional basketball player Adam Morrison (center) is a newsmaker who has diabetes. Others include actresses Halle Berry, Mary Tyler Moore, and Aida Turturro; author Anne Rice; composer Andrew Lloyd Webber; and Iron Man triathlete David Weingard.

But conditions in the environment, such as lack of exercise and poor diet, contribute to development of type 2 diabetes. Other studies are exploring genes that influence obesity as a risk factor for diabetes.

**Gender and Ethnic Background**

Diabetes affects males and females equally and occurs in every nationality. But some ethnic groups are more prone to the disease. For example, whites, especially from northern European countries, exhibit higher rates of type 1 diabetes than African Americans, American Indians, and Asians. In contrast, nonwhites face a greater risk of developing type 2 diabetes than whites do. Compared with whites, African Americans encounter 1.8 times the risk, while Hispanic and Latino groups experience 1.7 times and American Indians 2.2 times the risk.

Asians of Far Eastern descent—including Chinese, Korean, and Japanese people—are particularly prone to type 2 diabetes. The threat is greater for recent immigrants to the United States. They may have led a more physically demanding lifestyle and eaten a lower-fat diet in their native country. In the United States, they face a culture that encourages inactivity and a high-fat, sugar-laden diet. "When they give you the visa to the United States in Shanghai, Fujian or Beijing, [China], they should stamp a clear warning: danger to your health," said Marcelo Suarez-Orozco, codirector of immigration studies at New York University.

**Weight**

Weight plays an important role in type 2 diabetes. Eight out of ten people with this form of diabetes are overweight. In a national study of 122,000 women, those who gained between 11 and 18 pounds (5 to 8 kilograms) over a fourteen-year period were nearly twice as likely to develop diabetes as women who gained less than 11 pounds during the same period. Women who gained between 24 and 44 pounds (11 to 20 kg) had five times the risk of developing diabetes.

Being overweight increases your risk of diabetes, especially if you carry extra weight around your middle—an "apple" figure—rather than lower on the hips. Fat cells are less able than muscle cells to accept signals from insulin. Fat cells in the abdomen release fat into the bloodstream more easily than fat cells elsewhere, which contributes to insulin resistance.

**Lack of Physical Activity**
Lack of physical activity adds to weight problems and an increased risk of type 2 diabetes. Exercise burns unused calories from food you eat and drink. Extra calories that aren't burned are stored as fat.

Young people often spend much of their time in front of the television, computer, or video games at the expense of physical activities. Schools have added to the problem by cutting recess and physical education. As a result, many kids exercise too little. They face an increased risk of obesity and type 2 diabetes.

**Age**
The risk of diabetes grows as you age. About one in five people over the age of sixty-five has type 2 diabetes. As people grow older, their bodies change and they burn fewer calories. Yet most people tend to eat the same amount and exercise less. Weight gain and loss of muscle mass increases the risk of type 2 diabetes.

**Other Triggers**
Diabetes may develop following an illness or use of a medication that interrupts insulin production. Diabetes can result from infection, malnutrition, surgery, hydrocortisone drug treatment, and disorders of the pancreas, adrenal gland, and pituitary gland. As scientists continue to investigate the causes of diabetes, they try to educate the public about risk factors for the disease and healthy lifestyles to reduce the threat.

*Chapter 3*

# DETECTING DIABETES

## Sam's Story

*When Sam was in his thirties, he was diagnosed with type 2 diabetes. Back in the 1950s, however, doctors didn't pay much attention to high sugar levels unless the patient reported symptoms. Sam watched his weight and stayed slim, but he rarely checked his glucose levels or watched what he ate. At the age of seventy-four, however, Sam began to feel a tickling sensation in his legs. He went to a new doctor, who determined that high blood sugar levels had damaged nerves in Sam's legs. This doctor immediately prescribed drugs to control Sam's sugar levels.*

*Sam learned how to measure his blood sugar levels at home. By eating a balanced diet and taking his medication, he was able to keep his sugar levels in a healthy range. He spent more time taking care of himself, but he believed it was worth it to feel good and stay healthy enough to enjoy his retirement.*

Over time, high levels of sugar in the blood can create major problems, harming organs throughout the body. The longer diabetes goes undetected, the more damage it can cause. Testing blood sugar as part of a regular checkup can help doctors and their patients discover the disease early and begin treatment. Once a diagnosis is made, the goal is to keep blood sugar levels within a normal range as much as possible. This requires consistent home blood sugar testing.

## BLOOD SUGAR LEVELS

The amount of sugar circulating in your bloodstream naturally varies throughout the day, but it stays within a narrow limit. Normally, if you haven't eaten overnight, your blood glucose level the next morning measures between 70 to 100 milligrams per deciliter (mg/dl) of blood. That figure is equivalent to 1 teaspoon of sugar per gallon of water.

Anything outside this range spells trouble. A blood glucose measurement higher than 100 mg/dl following an overnight fast signals *hyperglycemia*, or high blood sugar. Glucose levels below 70 mg/dl indicate *hypoglycemia*, or low blood sugar. Both extremes cause a variety of symptoms and can lead to serious illness or death.

## TESTING FOR DIABETES

Doctors identify and monitor diabetes through tests that measure glucose levels in the blood.

### Fasting Plasma Glucose Test

The *fasting plasma glucose test* is easy to perform and the most reliable. The patient does not eat or drink anything except water for eight to twelve hours before the test. At the clinic, a blood sample is drawn from a vein in the patient's arm. A laboratory technician measures the amount of glucose in the *plasma*, the fluid part of the blood. A normal glucose level after fasting is between 70 mg/dl and 100 mg/dl. If the test shows a level higher than 125 mg/dl, doctors suspect diabetes. They usually order a second fasting glucose test to confirm results before making a firm diagnosis.

### Random Plasma Glucose Test

This test mirrors the fasting plasma test, but it measures blood sugar at any time, without a period of fasting first. A random test may be done as part of routine blood work during a physical exam. If test results show glucose levels of

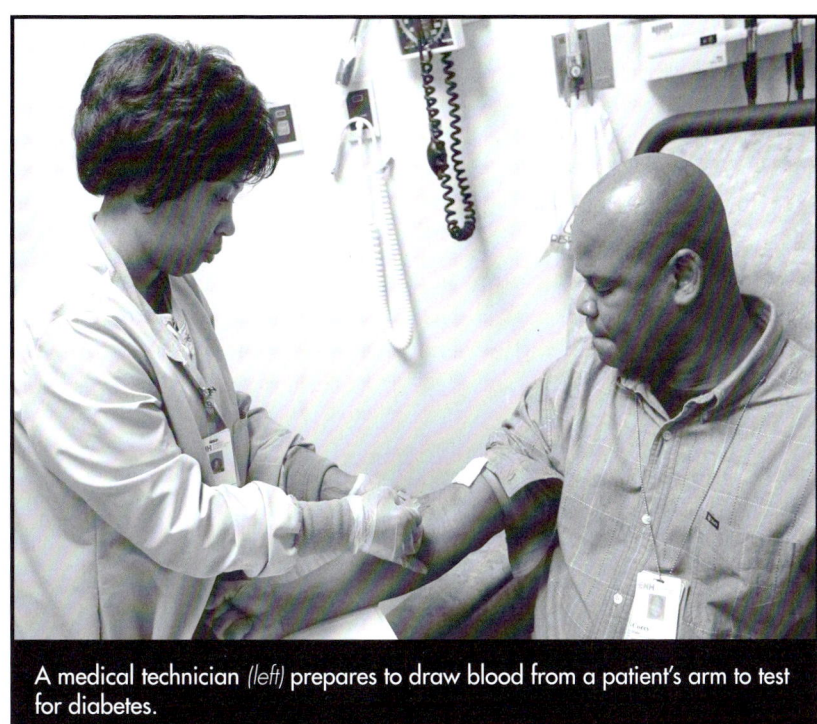

A medical technician (left) prepares to draw blood from a patient's arm to test for diabetes.

200 mg/dl or higher, doctors check further for diabetes. Most doctors recommend a fasting glucose test on another day to confirm the results.

### Oral Glucose Tolerance Test

Doctors recommend the oral *glucose tolerance test*, also known as a glucose challenge test, less frequently. This test is more time-consuming, costly, and difficult to administer than a fasting blood sugar test for much of the population. But doctors prefer the accuracy of the oral glucose test to detect gestational diabetes in pregnant women.

With an oral glucose test, the patient fasts for at least eight hours. After the fast, the patient first has blood drawn, then drinks 1 cup (0.3 liter) of very sweet liquid. The liquid contains 2.6 ounces (75 grams) of sugary-tasting glucose, about three times the amount of sweetener in soft drinks. A technician measures blood sugar once an hour for the next three hours. Multiple test results show how the pancreas handles excess sugar over time. Glucose levels that rise or fall too much signal trouble. If glucose levels climb more than expected and do not return to normal by the third hour, the patient likely has diabetes.

### Glycosylated Hemoglobin (A1C) Test

This test is used to assess blood sugar control over a period of two to three months. It helps doctors and patients know how well treatment is working. A1C results show what percentage of hemoglobin—a protein in red blood cells—is sugar coated, or glycosylated. The goal for people with diabetes is less than 7 percent.

## PREDIABETES

Sometimes test results show glucose levels that are above normal but not high enough to qualify as diabetes. Borderline high blood sugar levels indicate a condition known as prediabetes. Having prediabetes raises your risk of developing type 2 diabetes.

A diagnosis of prediabetes, also called glucose impairment, may be based on results from either the fasting glucose or oral glucose tolerance test. Impaired fasting glucose (IFG) means that blood sugar levels are between 100 and 125 mg/dl after fasting overnight. Impaired glucose tolerance (IGT) refers to glucose levels between 140 and 199 mg/dl after two hours during the oral glucose tolerance test.

The U.S. government estimates that 40 percent of Americans ages 40 to 74—about 41 million people—currently test in the prediabetic range. Many of them will develop type 2 diabetes within the next ten years.

People with prediabetes can take action to prevent full-blown diabetes from developing. The most important steps are to lose weight, choose healthier foods, and exercise regularly. According to the National Institute of Diabetes and Digestive and Kidney Diseases, the risk of diabetes drops after losing 5 to 7 percent of body weight through diet and increased physical activity. In one study, three thousand people with impaired glucose tolerance lost 10 to 14 pounds (5 to 6 kg) and walked at least thirty minutes each day for five days each week. They reduced their risk of diabetes by almost 60 percent. Another group in the same study took medication but did not follow the diet and exercise program. Results for this group revealed only half the success (31 percent reduced risk).

## THE DIABETES CARE TEAM

After a diagnosis of diabetes, the next step is to gather information. People with diabetes have a lot to learn about their disease and treatment. Anyone with a serious, long-term disease such as diabetes needs support to help manage the condition and stick with a treatment plan.

People with diabetes benefit from regular visits to their family doctor as well as various specialists—physicians who concentrate on a particular area of medicine, such as feet or eye health. In some cities, doctors send newly diagnosed patients to training sessions at a hospital, clinic, or doctor's office. In these classes, people with diabetes meet several health-care professionals who help them learn to take charge of their treatment and their health.

## Endocrinologist

An *endocrinologist* is a medical doctor trained to identify and treat disorders of the endocrine system—the glands and organs that secrete hormones into the bloodstream. One of these glands is the pancreas, which produces insulin. Endocrinologists test for diabetes, determine the type and extent of the disease, and recommend treatment. Children and adolescents with diabetes should see a pediatric endocrinologist (an endocrinologist who treats young people) every three months for optimal care.

## Diabetes Educator

A diabetes educator explains what diabetes is and answers questions about living with the disease. Diabetes educators train patients to monitor, or check, their blood sugar with a *blood sugar meter* and establish a routine for checking regularly. Patients learn to watch for symptoms of high or low blood sugar. For people who take insulin, a diabetes educator shows them how to inject the drug and adjust doses. Diabetes educators usually work as registered nurses, *dieticians*, or pharmacists before receiving special training in diabetes. They see patients in doctor's offices, hospitals, or clinics.

"I went to the hospital for a couple days, and the diabetes educator gave me a thorough grounding in what diabetes is and how to manage it," Jared says.

## Dietician or Nutritionist

Dieticians, or nutritionists, teach patients how to control their blood sugar and weight through diet. They work with patients to plan a balanced diet they feel comfortable following. A dietician provides information about measur-

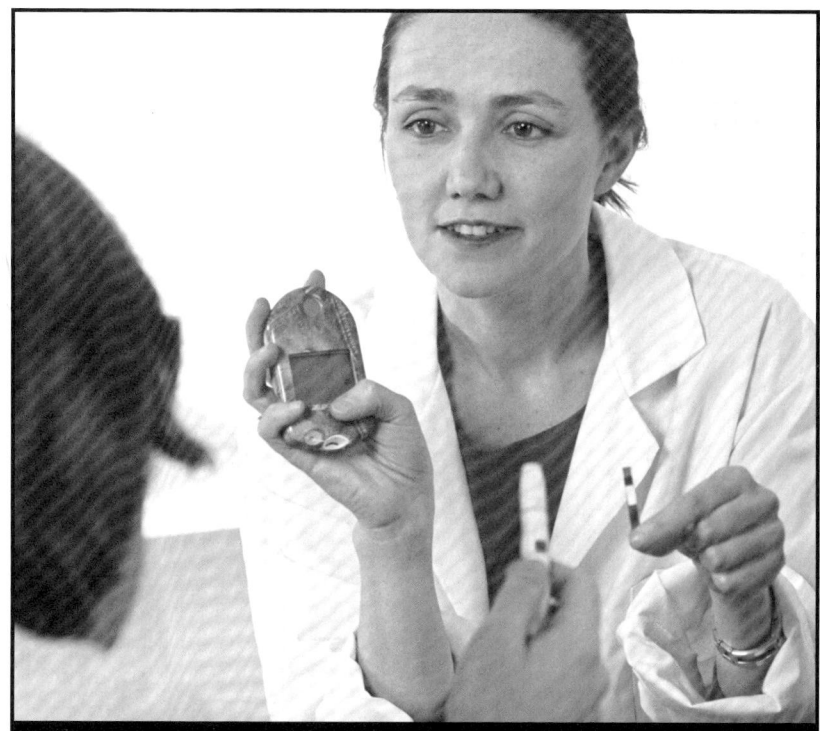
A diabetes educator can help people who are newly diagnosed feel less overwhelmed as they learn what their treatment involves.

ing portion sizes and balancing amounts of nutrients in meals.

"The dietician talked about maintaining a healthy diet," Shawna remembers. "In the beginning, I was a lot stricter with following my diet. After a while, I learned to estimate food and insulin amounts."

**Other Specialists**
Because high blood sugar can cause damage in several parts of the body, people with diabetes need to see several different health professionals regularly. Ophthalmologists

examine eyes to prevent diabetes-related vision problems. Podiatrists, or foot doctors, check feet for poor blood circulation and sores that can lead to infection. Foot doctors teach patients how to trim their toenails and deal with corns and calluses. People with diabetes may see a dermatologist, or skin doctor, to treat skin infections, while regular visits to the dentist help them prevent mouth-related problems.

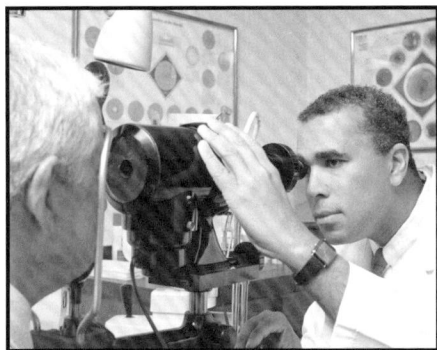

It is important for people with diabetes to get annual eye exams. The earlier a problem is caught, the easier it is to correct.

## LEADING THE DIABETES CARE TEAM

In the end, the patient is the most important person on the care team. If you have diabetes, even as a young person, it's up to you to take charge of your treatment. You are the team leader. The first step is to admit you have a chronic illness that will require your attention for the rest of your life. Then you must be willing to follow your treatment program. This usually means making changes in your diet and physical activities. You can get help, support, and guidance from a diabetes care team or through agencies, such as the American Diabetes Association (see "Resources" on page 106). But diabetes is a personal journey, one that is guided by the person with diabetes.

*Chapter 4*

# TAKING CONTROL

## Jim's Story

*Jim is a retired doctor who has type 2 diabetes. He wants to avoid complications from the disease, so he watches his blood sugar levels carefully. He tests his blood every morning and two hours after he eats. Jim's blood sugar meter shows the date, time, and blood sugar measurement. He records these figures in a log to take to his doctor.*

*Jim also follows a meal plan that emphasizes whole grains, vegetables, lean sources of protein, and fruits. He walks an hour most days. With the help of a healthy eating and activity plan and regular visits with his health-care team, he keeps his diabetes from getting worse and damaging other parts of his body.*

## TREATMENT BASICS

In the past, having diabetes guaranteed a shortened life. That's because uncontrolled diabetes can cause a host of problems, or complications, including high *blood pressure*, heart disease, kidney failure, blindness, loss of limbs, and nerve damage. But advances in diabetes care have improved the outlook for people with diabetes. Patients who keep their sugar levels in balance can expect to live long, healthy, and active lives. They learn to plan ahead, exercise, and control what they eat.

"Treatment has changed a lot since 1993 when Jared was diagnosed," says his mother, Ann. "There are new meters for measuring blood sugar and long-acting and short-acting insulin. With tight control of blood sugar, people with diabetes can help stave off problems."

The main focus of treatment is to keep blood glucose levels within a normal range. This is key to preventing symptoms and complications. To maintain healthy blood sugar levels, patients must follow a multifaceted plan.

Learning what to do and staying on course can be challenging. Many people rely on a diabetes care team, peer support group, or online support group to help them adjust to lifestyle changes diabetes requires. The mainstays of treatment are a healthy diet, weight control, physical activity, and regular blood glucose testing.

## CHOOSING FOODS

Food you eat contributes to your overall health. You get energy and vitamins and minerals by eating a mix of *carbohydrates*, proteins, and fats. Dieticians recommend a diet that includes a variety of foods offering a healthy balance of nutrients. This is true whether or not you have diabetes. But food selection, portion size, and timing of meals become more important if you have diabetes. What you eat, how much you eat, and when you eat all affect glucose levels.

At one time, doctors told patients with diabetes to stop eating all sweets and follow a prescribed diet. Sugary snacks were thought to make glucose levels rise too much. More recently, scientists have discovered that a person's reaction to different foods depends on several factors. Does one food, even within the same food group, cause blood sugar levels to spike more than another? How large a portion triggers a reaction? Was the sugary food eaten in combination with other foods? All these elements may be considered when planning a healthy diet for someone with diabetes.

For a person with diabetes, meals resemble science experiments. What combinations of foods work best to avoid a high or low blood sugar level?

**Carbohydrates**

Carbohydrates supply the body's main source of fuel for energy. *Simple carbohydrates* are found in fruits, milk and milk products, refined white flour, and sweets, such as candy, table sugar, cake, and cookies. *Complex carbohydrates* form the basis of whole-grain products, including whole-wheat bread and brown rice, and are found in beans, peas, legumes, and starchy vegetables,

People newly diagnosed with diabetes are often surprised to learn that nutritious foods such as skim milk have carbohydrates in them.

such as potatoes and corn. Nonstarchy vegetables, such as broccoli, spinach, zucchini, and lettuce, are carbohydrates that are mostly *fiber*.

Fiber comes from the cells of plant walls, and it remains largely undigested. As such, it helps food pass through the digestive system. Fiber is thought to help control blood sugar by slowing absorption of other carbohydrates. When you eat oatmeal, green vegetables, and other plant-based products, they take longer to move through your digestive system. The result is a slower rise in blood glucose than from eating foods made of simple carbohydrates.

As an added bonus, complex carbohydrates and high-fiber foods make you feel full for longer and contain many important vitamins and minerals. They provide excellent nutrition, in contrast to refined sugars, such as candy, which lack vitamins, minerals, and fiber. Refined sugars are often called "empty calories" because they have little or no nutritional value. But they do have calories and can lead to weight gain.

People with diabetes find they maintain better control of blood sugar by eating a variety of complex carbohydrates and fiber-rich foods. In one study, participants reduced their blood sugar levels by about 10 percent by increasing their intake of high-fiber foods, such as broccoli, spinach, and whole-wheat breads, pastas, and cereals. Based on this and other studies, dieticians recommend a diet rich in fibrous foods to stabilize blood sugar levels. Nutrition experts recommend that carbohydrates make up between 40 and 60 percent of daily calories for most people.

### Carb Counting

Doctors often suggest counting carbohydrates, or "carbs," to plan meals, help maintain good blood sugar control, and determine how much insulin to take. One carb serving is equal to 15 grams of carbohydrates. To determine carb counts of various foods, you can buy one of several booklets that provide carb listings, check carb-counting websites, or read the nutrition facts label on food packages.

When you read food labels, focus on total carbohydrates and serving size. For example, one-half cup of bran cereal may contain 23 total carbs. Think about how many servings you might eat and whether you would add milk, sugar, or fruit. Then add the total amount of carbs for everything. Insulin users count carbs to determine their insulin dose for a meal. For those who do not require insulin, counting carbohydrates is a way to calculate how many servings are in a meal or snack to keep the day's eating in balance. Although carb counting may seem daunting at first, learning average carbs per food becomes second nature with some practice.

**Proteins and Fats**
Another way to help keep glucose levels steady is to combine carbohydrates with proteins and fats, the two other main food groups. Proteins include meat, poultry, seafood, eggs, nuts, beans, soy products, and legumes. The body uses proteins to build and repair tissues. When you eat proteins with carbohydrates, your digestion slows down and your blood glucose levels rise more slowly than if you eat carbs alone.

Protein-rich foods are important for a healthy, balanced diet. But too much protein can contribute to kidney problems and weight gain from excess calories. Dieticians suggest that 10 to 20 percent of daily calories should come from protein.

Fats are found in animal products, such as meat, fish, and dairy products, and plant foods such as nuts, avocados, and olives. Although low-fat diets and products get a lot of attention, the body needs some fat. Fats provide a source of stored energy. Without some fat in your diet, your body burns tissue and muscle for food. But eating too much fat or too much of the wrong kind of fat increases the likelihood of weight gain, which can lead to type 2 diabetes.

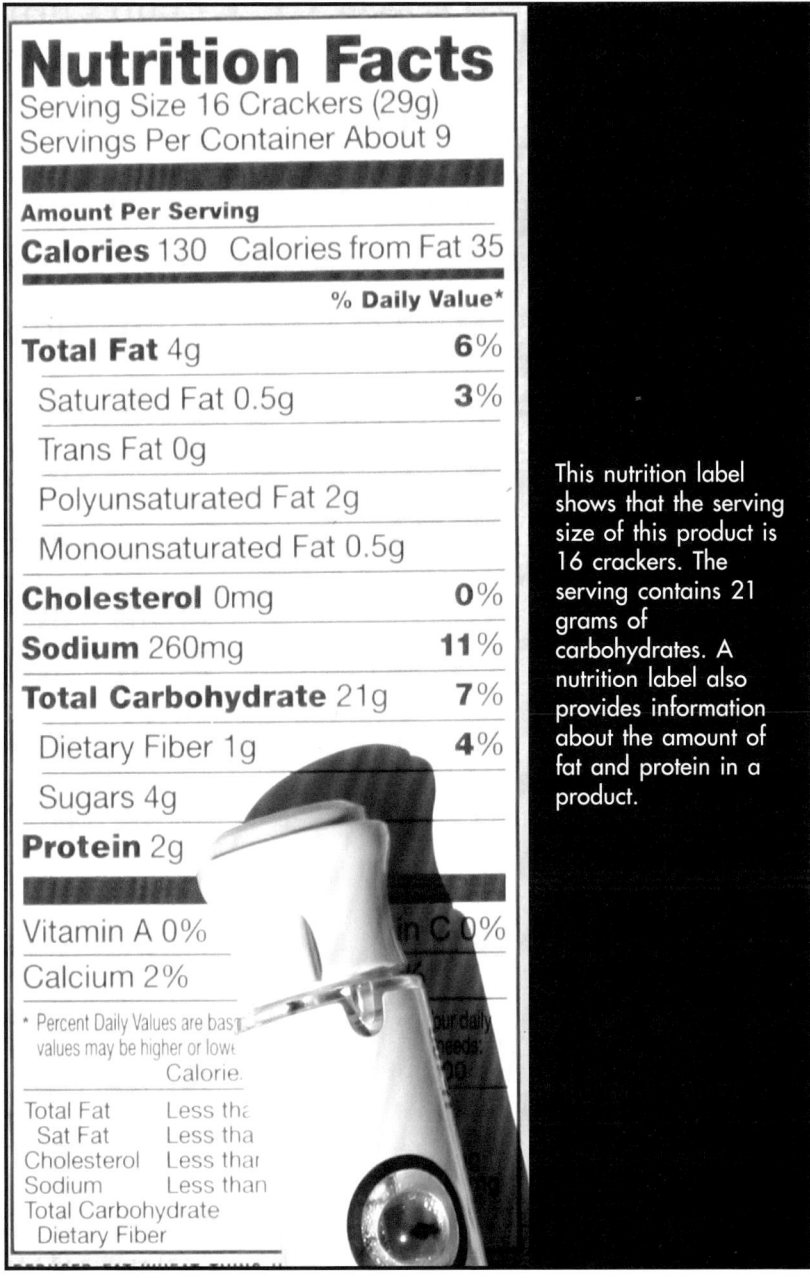

# Nutrition Facts

Serving Size 16 Crackers (29g)
Servings Per Container About 9

**Amount Per Serving**

**Calories** 130   Calories from Fat 35

% Daily Value*

| | |
|---|---|
| **Total Fat** 4g | 6% |
| Saturated Fat 0.5g | 3% |
| Trans Fat 0g | |
| Polyunsaturated Fat 2g | |
| Monounsaturated Fat 0.5g | |
| **Cholesterol** 0mg | 0% |
| **Sodium** 260mg | 11% |
| **Total Carbohydrate** 21g | 7% |
| Dietary Fiber 1g | 4% |
| Sugars 4g | |
| **Protein** 2g | |

Vitamin A 0%        Vitamin C 0%

Calcium 2%

* Percent Daily Values are bas___
  values may be higher or lowe___
                   Calorie___

Total Fat          Less tha___
  Sat Fat          Less tha___
Cholesterol        Less thar___
Sodium             Less than___
Total Carbohydrate
  Dietary Fiber

This nutrition label shows that the serving size of this product is 16 crackers. The serving contains 21 grams of carbohydrates. A nutrition label also provides information about the amount of fat and protein in a product.

Health professionals recommend that no more than 30 percent of your total calories each day come from fats. Less than one-third of your fat calories should come from foods made from animals, such as meat and dairy products. Healthier sources of fat can be found in fish and fish oils, seeds and nuts, and vegetable oils, such as canola, olive, and soybean.

## HOW MANY CALORIES DO YOU NEED?

Calories are a measurement of energy produced from food that the body uses. Most energy from food is released as heat to control body temperature. A calorie is a measure of that heat. Carbohydrates, proteins, and fats each produce different amounts of energy, or calories. Fats have 9 calories per gram, while proteins and carbohydrates each have 4 calories per gram.

If you consume more calories than you burn, the unused calories are stored as fat. That's why it's important to eat within the recommended number of calories each day. Daily calorie guidelines established by the U.S. Department of Agriculture differ according to a person's age and activity level.

| | |
|---|---|
| Children ages 2–6 | 1,600 calories per day |
| Inactive women | 1,600 calories per day |
| Older adults | 1,600 calories per day |
| Children ages 7–12 | 2,200 calories per day |
| Teenage girls | 2,200 calories per day |
| Active women | 2,200 calories per day |
| Inactive men | 2,200 calories per day |
| Teenage boys | 2,800 calories per day |
| Active men | 2,800 calories per day |

## CREATING A MEAL PLAN

Many people with diabetes find it helpful to follow a meal plan—a set of guidelines for eating a variety of foods. Within these guidelines, you can choose your favorite foods and decide how much to eat.

Every meal plan is different. For example, people who are overweight may want a plan that includes meals and snacks throughout the day but provides fewer calories overall. Or insulin users need to balance food choices and times with the amount of insulin and exercise they take.

"I became more aware of what I ate and how it affected me after learning I had diabetes," says Emily, Jared's younger sister, who also has diabetes. "I've been to a dietician several times, and we adjust my meal plan. It helps to have a meal plan because then I know how much insulin to take."

A meal plan begins with keeping a log of everything you eat and any reactions these foods cause. A log helps people with diabetes and their dietician choose foods and meal times that ensure stable blood glucose levels. Some people with diabetes can eat three meals a day without snacking and keep their blood sugar levels in control. Others require several smaller meals and snacks between meals. A complete log can help determine correct portion sizes and the healthiest balance of carbohydrates, proteins, and fats.

One of the most difficult parts of meal planning is determining the right portion size. In the United States, a culture of "more is better" has led to gigantic serving sizes in restaurants and packaged food. Portions have doubled or tripled compared with what people ate thirty years ago. Many Americans are accustomed to these large servings. But large portions pack added calories and contribute to weight gain and soaring blood sugar levels. Choosing smaller serving sizes helps with weight loss and diabetes management.

# RATE YOUR PLATE

The American Diabetes Association created an easy way to figure out the types and portions of foods to eat at each meal. The organization calls it "Rate Your Plate." The ADA suggests picturing each meal as a dinner plate divided into halves, with one half split into two sections:

- One-fourth of the plate includes grains or starchy foods, such as rice, pasta, potatoes, or corn.
- One-fourth holds proteins, such as meat, fish, poultry, meat substitute, tofu, or beans.
- One-half is covered with salads or nonstarchy vegetables, such as lettuce, tomatoes, broccoli, cucumbers, cauliflower, green and red peppers, and artichokes.

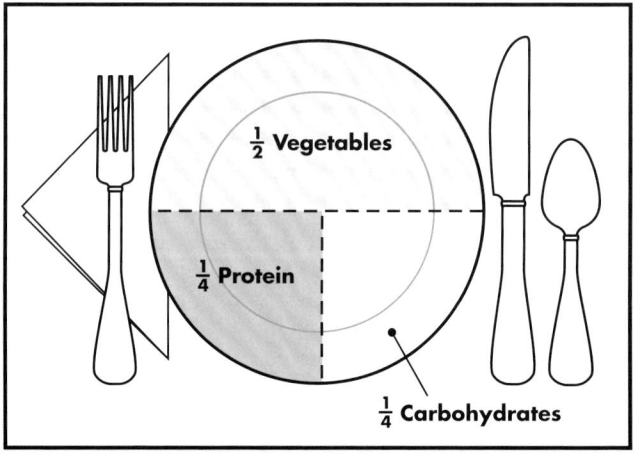

*Copyright © 2007 American Diabetes Association*
*From http://www.diabetes.org*
*Reprinted with permission from The American Diabetes Association*

Diabetes educators recommend eating whole fruits rather than drinking fruit juice. Whole fruits are digested more slowly and create a longer-lasting full feeling.

### FOOD EXCHANGES

Food exchanges are another option, much like carb counting, for helping people newly diagnosed with diabetes make healthier food choices. Exchanges divide food choices into categories: vegetables, fruits, fats, milk products, and meats or meat substitutes. The plan allows for a given number of servings or choices from each food group at every meal. The number of servings from a given group depends on individual goals for limiting calories or carbohydrates and providing a nutritional balance.

Within each food group are a number of choices, called exchanges. Each choice, or exchange, offers similar nutrients and effects on blood sugar. The idea that one food can be exchanged for another helps with planning healthy, varied meals. The American Diabetes Association offers materials that identify exchanges for meal planning.

## WATCHING WHAT YOU EAT

Besides preparing and implementing a meal plan, people with (and without) diabetes can follow other simple suggestions to make healthier food choices.

### Read Food Labels

One of the best ways to improve your health is to read the labels on food packages. Federal guidelines require companies to print nutrition information on most food packaging. Nutrition facts usually include the amount of calories, carbohydrates, fats, protein, and fiber in an item, along with percentages of daily vitamin requirements one portion meets.

Equally important, nutrition labels list the product's ingredients. Manufacturers list ingredients according to weight, so those listed first make up the bulk of the product. Ingredients at the end of the list represent the smallest proportion of the item.

Nutrition facts can help people with diabetes decide which foods and in what amounts fit into their overall program. Labels describe what manufacturers calculate as a single portion size, which can help with meal planning. But keep in mind that the stated portion size may differ from an exchange serving size or a healthy portion for a particular meal plan.

## DO THE MATH

People in good control of their diabetes do a lot of math. For example, the serving size on a nutrition label shows that 5 pieces total 22 grams of carbohydrate per serving. Someone with diabetes needs to calculate the number of pieces in a standard 15-gram serving size on a diabetic meal plan. The answer is between 3 pieces, or 13.2 grams, and 4 pieces, or 17.6 grams. Ten pieces, or 44 grams, are three servings.

Consumers also need to pay attention to health claims on food packaging. Food manufacturers sometimes print paid endorsements from health-related organizations or make misleading statements about a food's nutritional value. The best way to understand what you're buying and eating is to read the nutrition facts panel carefully.

**Eat Colorful Foods**

Another tool for making healthy food choices involves eating a variety of colorful foods. A colorful plate includes an array of fruits, vegetables, grains, dairy products, and meats. Brightly colored fruits and vegetables—apples, bananas, broccoli, squash, eggplant, blueberries, and more—help keep blood sugar highs and lows in check.

Healthy portions of a variety of foods is important to successful blood sugar control.

In one study of people with type 2 diabetes, half the participants ate a vegan diet, which centered on fruits, vegetables, beans, and grains and avoided meats, added fats, and dairy products. The other half of participants followed a diet that included small amounts of animal products, such as meat and butter. Results showed that 43 percent of participants on the vegan diet reduced the amount of diabetes medication they took, compared with 26 percent on the other diet. The vegan group doubled their weight loss—14 pounds (6 kg) compared with 7 pounds (3 kg)—and tested with more stable blood sugar levels.

**Choose Water-Dense Foods**
Another tip for a healthier diet is to eat foods loaded with water, including fruits, vegetables, and cooked whole grains. Foods with a high water content pack fewer calories into larger quantities, so you can eat more and feel full with fewer calories. The full feeling comes from water and fiber that fill your stomach quicker. A full stomach suppresses appetite and helps with weight loss and diabetes control.

**Avoid Alcohol**
Drinking alcohol often spells trouble for people with diabetes. Alcohol can cause blood sugar levels to drop or rise, depending on the individual and type of drink. Combining alcohol with medication or insulin to lower blood sugar levels may result in hypoglycemia.

If adults with diabetes choose to drink, they should do so in moderation and take care in choosing alcoholic beverages. Sugary drinks, such as sweet wines, wine coolers, and alcohol mixed with juices, contain higher amounts of sugar and carbohydrates that may increase blood glucose levels too much and too quickly. Another way to keep glucose levels in check is to eat before and while drinking. Food absorbs and balances some of the effects of alcohol.

## KEEP MOVING

"Diabetes can be helped by lifestyle choices. It makes you take charge of your lifestyle and be extra healthy to cope with it effectively," Jared says. "I exercise. I ride my bicycle a lot. I play basketball. I do *yoga*. I jog."

Physical exercise can help prevent and control diabetes. Exercise promotes weight loss and helps the body convert sugar to fuel. In addition, people who stay physically active enjoy better health overall. A boost in physical activity of any kind translates into more energy, longer life, and less risk of illness, including heart disease, high blood pressure, and osteoporosis, a bone disease.

When you exercise, your muscles contract (tighten) and relax. To do this, they use glucose from the bloodstream for energy. At the same time, moderate prolonged activity, such as swimming or jogging, signals the liver to release glycogen into the bloodstream. The glycogen makes cells more sensitive to insulin. As the body uses glycogen for energy, blood sugar levels fall. The stabilizing effect continues for hours after physical activity.

Exercise offers many benefits for people with diabetes. It helps stabilize blood sugar and hormones that influence mood. It also strengthens the heart, lungs, bones, and joints.

A regular exercise program gives people a powerful tool for managing their own health and well-being. According to Dr. Richard K. Bernstein, author of *Dr. Bernstein's Diabetes Solution*, "Type 1 diabetics who engage in a regular exercise program tend to take better care of their blood sugars and diet." For people with type 2 diabetes, exercise contributes to better glucose control and a reduced need for medication or insulin. For those with prediabetes, exercise decreases the likelihood of developing type 2 diabetes.

The American Diabetes Association recommends exercising for thirty to sixty minutes most days each week. Find one or more activities that are fun or satisfying enough to hold your interest over time. Your activity need not be strenuous. The best blood sugar control results from extended, moderate activity. Be sure to wear comfortable footwear and polyester or cotton-polyester socks to prevent blisters and keep your feet dry. In hot weather, drink water before and during exercise. Because exercise affects blood sugar levels, ask your diabetes care team about when to check your blood sugar and coordinate your insulin or medication with the physical activity.

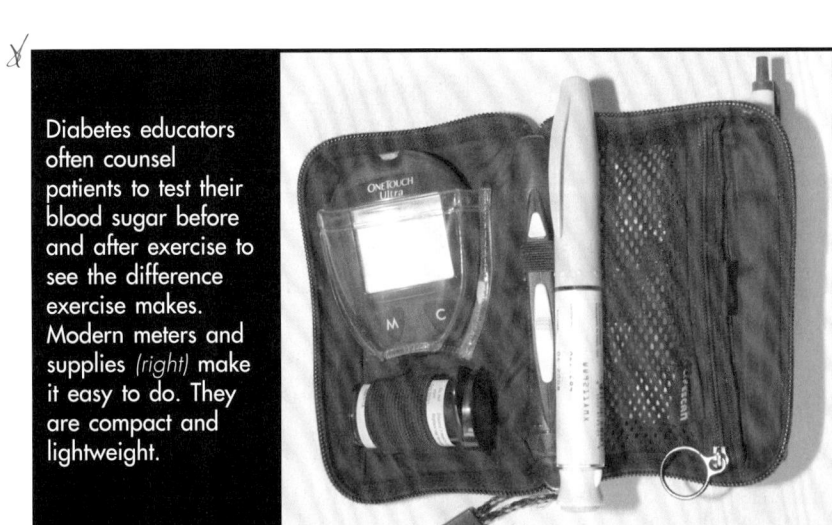

Diabetes educators often counsel patients to test their blood sugar before and after exercise to see the difference exercise makes. Modern meters and supplies (right) make it easy to do. They are compact and lightweight.

## MONITORING BLOOD SUGAR

Diabetes interferes with the body's natural ability to identify and regulate blood sugar levels. Therefore, patients must monitor their glucose levels with a meter. The only way to know if blood sugar levels are within a safe range is to check them regularly. Monitoring helps guide treatment plans and decisions about medication, diet, and activity.

### Drawing Blood Samples

Blood glucose testing relies on measuring samples of blood. A variety of blood sugar meters are available. Most read plasma in a drop of blood. To get the blood sample, you use a *lancet* to prick the side of your finger. A lancet is a sharp, fine needle. Lancets come in spring-loaded devices that look like a pen. They are easy to use and cause little pain. Some meters allow you to draw blood from a site other than the finger, such as your palm or forearm. Other blood glucose meters also serve as insulin injection pens.

In the early twenty-first century, a newer testing device, called a *continuous glucose monitor (CGM)* measures glucose levels in *interstitial fluid*, the clear fluid under the skin that carries glucose and other nutrients from the bloodstream to the cells. Some continuous monitors use a tiny sensor inserted beneath the skin. The sensor transmits blood glucose information to a monitor worn on a belt or in a pocket. The sensor can stay under the skin for up to three days before it must be replaced. Another device is a continuous glucose monitoring patch, worn on top of the skin.

Most continuous blood glucose monitors measure levels every few minutes. Frequent reports alert users to where levels are headed. Some monitors sound an alarm when blood sugar goes too high or too low. With this added information, someone with diabetes may choose to eat a snack or stop exercising to stop a dangerously low blood sugar level. To avert a damaging high, the person may choose to get some exercise or reduce the carb count of the next meal.

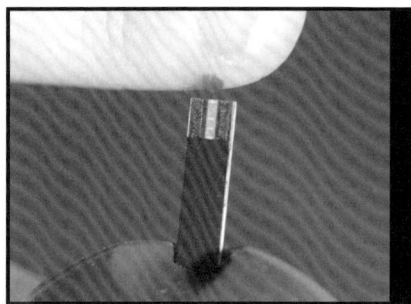

A test strip requires a tiny drop of blood, but it is still a wound. To minimize soreness, people with diabetes stick the sides rather than the pads of their fingertips and follow a routine rotation of test sites.

## Measuring Blood Samples

To measure glucose in a drop of blood, you put it on a test strip, a chemically treated strip that goes into a blood sugar meter. The meter quickly measures and displays glucose levels in the blood sample. Blood sugar meters contain small computers that process and store information. Depending upon the amount of memory the meter has, it may store results for several weeks. Some meters allow you to download data onto your personal computer and track blood sugar trends over time.

A range of lightweight, palm-sized meters is available in different sizes and colors. Special versions offer larger screens for easy viewing and talking meters for those who are visually impaired.

## Recording in a Diary or Log

Doctors encourage patients to record their test results in a log or diary. Tracking the numbers lets you see how various foods, activities, medications, illness, and other situations affect your blood sugar. The American Diabetes Association sells a color-coded desk diabetes management planner that highlights daily food intake, testing results, medication, and exercise. A log helps you and your diabetes care team evaluate a new treatment routine or change in medication. As one man with diabetes said, "No news is not good news as a diabetic. The more we know about our condition, the better our condition."

## Blood Glucose, Food/Activity, and Insulin Dosage Record    Date _____

| BREAKFAST | | | | | SNACK | LUNCH | | | | | SNACK | SUPPER | | | | | SNACK | | |
|---|---|---|---|---|---|---|---|---|---|---|---|---|---|---|---|---|---|---|---|
| Pre | | Dose | 2-hr Post | | | Pre | | Dose | 2-hr Post | | | Pre | | Dose | 2-hr Post | | | Bedtime | Overnight |
| Time | BG | H __ + __ Total __ | Time | BG | | Time | BG | H __ + __ Total __ | Time | BG | | Time | BG | H __ + __ Total __ | Time | BG | Dose H __ | BG Time | BG Time |

ACTIVITY

_____ grams = _____ choices          _____ gms _____ chos          _____ grams = _____ choices          _____ gms _____ chos          _____ grams = _____ choices          _____ gms _____ chos

NOTES

BLOOD PRESSURE
BEFORE ____/____
AFTER ____/____

---

**This daily record page for insulin users includes plenty of room to note meals, activities, and other details important to good diabetes self-management.**

*Chapter 5*

# MEDICATIONS AND INSULIN

## Emily's Story

*Emily, aged twenty-four, was sixteen when she found out she had type 1 diabetes. "My parents both have first cousins with type 1 diabetes, and so does my brother," she says. "Before I was diagnosed, our family gave blood as part of a diabetes study. Test results found evidence of an antibody that indicated I had a good chance of developing diabetes. Two years after the test, I received the diagnosis."*

*Because her pancreas was producing almost no insulin, Emily started taking insulin right away. "I had to be careful about what I was eating because I didn't know how to measure my blood sugar," she recalls. "Figuring out the right amount of insulin to take is a balancing act, a lot of trial and error. So the first weekend, I worked with the doctors a lot."*

*Over time, Emily became adept at measuring her blood sugar levels and understanding how to change her insulin dosage based on what she eats and her activities. She uses both long-acting and rapid-acting forms of the hormone-based medication.*

## THE NEXT LEVEL OF TREATMENT

Many people with type 2 diabetes can control their glucose levels through diet, weight loss, exercise, and blood sugar monitoring. Others must take medication or inject insulin to keep blood sugar levels stable. People with type 1 diabetes need to include insulin in their treatment plan.

Medications are not miracle cures. Often patients and doctors must balance a drug's benefits and side effects. Some medications work better when taken in combination with other drugs. Even if a treatment plan includes medications, diet and exercise still play key roles in staying healthy and helping obtain better results from medication.

## DIABETES DRUGS

If diet and exercise fail to keep glucose levels stable in people with type 2 diabetes, doctors add medication to the treatment plan. The type of drug and how often it is taken depend on different factors. How much do blood sugar levels need to be lowered? How old is the patient? What other medications is the person taking? Can the patient handle possible side effects from a specific medicine?

Several classes of drugs can help produce stable blood sugar levels. Each type acts differently to achieve similar results. Sulfonylureas—such as glipizide (Glucotrol), glyburide (DiaBeta, Glynase, and Micronase) and glimepiride (Amaryl)—stimulate the pancreas to manufacture more insulin. In turn, the extra insulin lowers blood glucose levels.

People who benefit from this type of drug are normal weight, take small amounts of insulin or none, and have had diabetes for less than five years. Side effects may include low blood sugar, nausea, skin rash, and headache.

Pills, called biguanides—metformin (Fortamet, Glucophage, and others)—act by slowing the release of stored glucose from the liver. At the same time, they make cells more sensitive to insulin. These medications increase the risk of liver or kidney damage, so people taking them must be checked regularly for signs of liver or kidney disease.

Alpha-glucosidase inhibitors—acarbose (Precose) and miglitol (Glyset)—keep the intestines from giving off hormones that break down sugar. This slows digestion and the body's ability to absorb sugar. Doctors recommend these drugs to people who experience elevated blood sugars after eating.

Researchers are constantly testing new and improved diabetes medications. In the early twenty-first century, two promising drugs are exenatide (Byetta) and sitagliptin phosphate (Januvia), which belong to a class of drugs known as incretin mimetics. Both stimulate insulin production while curbing the liver's release of sugar. A bonus is that they can help with weight loss. Most medications for type 2 diabetes cause weight gain—exactly what people with diabetes try to avoid. Patients who take these new drugs find they can maintain or lose weight while improving their blood sugar levels.

"I used to have a love affair with my refrigerator," said a man with diabetes after six months on Byetta. "Now I eat about half of what I used to eat. My numbers are good even for a nondiabetic now."

## TAKING INSULIN

Everyone with type 1 diabetes needs insulin to balance what their pancreas cannot make. In addition, about 30 percent of people with type 2 diabetes require insulin. For these patients, oral medications alone do not keep glucose levels steady.

Sometimes the medicine burdens the overworked pancreas to produce more insulin. As the pancreas works harder to meet demand, its ability to manufacture insulin slows or stops completely.

In the past, insulin was made from cow or pig pancreases. But animal insulin sometimes resulted in uneven absorption and allergic reactions. In response, scientists developed a synthetic, or artificial, insulin with a chemical makeup identical to that of human insulin. Most people who need insulin use this form.

Insulin must be injected with a tiny needle, delivered via a pump, or inhaled into the lungs. Pills do not work because stomach acids released during digestion break up and destroy the insulin before it reaches the bloodstream. These other ways of delivering insulin send it into the bloodstream without having to go through the stomach.

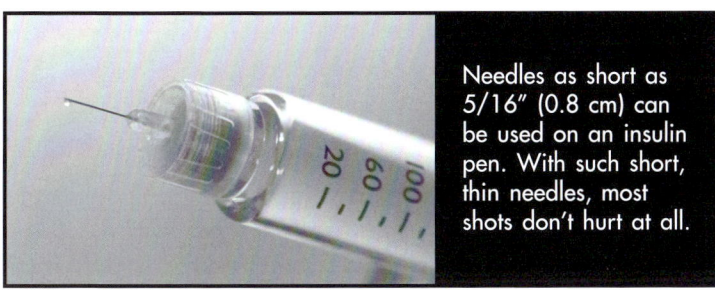

Needles as short as 5/16" (0.8 cm) can be used on an insulin pen. With such short, thin needles, most shots don't hurt at all.

### Types of Insulin

Doctors may prescribe one or more of several types of insulin. Each works at a different rate. Rapid, or fast-acting, insulin begins working within five to fifteen minutes. People take this form just before eating. If they inject fast-acting insulin and delay eating, blood sugar drops to dangerous levels.

Short-acting, or regular, insulin works thirty minutes after injection—the time the body needs to digest a meal.

Intermediate and long-acting insulins last longer in the system. Therefore, fewer injections are needed throughout the day. Still, people using these types must follow a regimented meal plan of eating certain amounts at certain times during the day. Rapid-acting insulin requires more injections but allows for more flexibility in eating choices and activity. Most people who require insulin take a long-acting insulin once or twice a day and use rapid-acting insulin before eating and to correct high blood sugars.

The types and amounts of insulin you need depend on many factors: your body size, how sensitive your cells are to small amounts of insulin produced by the pancreas, your activity level, and your food selections at each meal.

## HONEYMOON PHASE

Shortly after beginning to take insulin, many people with type 1 diabetes experience a sudden improvement. Blood sugar levels become stable, requiring less insulin to maintain good control. The improvement may last weeks, months, or a year. Doctors call this the honeymoon phase. But, just as a honeymoon ends and real married life begins, blood sugar problems return. Diabetes is a chronic illness that never goes away completely.

What causes this honeymoon phase? At the start of insulin treatment, the body may still be producing some insulin. Adding insulin by injection allows the pancreas beta cells to regain enough strength to meet the body's demand. Over time, however, the immune system continues attacking and destroying beta cells. Insulin production drops, and more insulin injections are needed to make up for the loss.

Requirements vary from one person to another. Some people get better results from short-acting insulin taken in smaller doses several times a day. Others respond better to longer-acting insulin. Many use both types.

Most people using insulin test their blood sugar six to eight times a day to determine how much insulin to take with food. "Once you know the amount of glucose, you can figure out how much insulin to take," Jared explains. "I test on average four times a day. A lot of times I know what a particular extreme, either high or low blood sugar, will feel like. I test my blood sugar, and if it confirms my thinking, I know how much insulin to inject."

Even with careful planning, your insulin program may need tweaking over time. The disease may improve or worsen, other health factors may develop, or new forms of insulin medication might become available. Researchers continue to look for ways to make insulin more effective and easier to administer.

### Injecting Insulin

To inject insulin, people with diabetes use a syringe with a needle attached, an insulin pen, or a jet injector. The most common method of insulin delivery is by syringe, especially if you mix two types of insulin. A pen injector looks like a fat marker. Users select the correct dose on a dial before

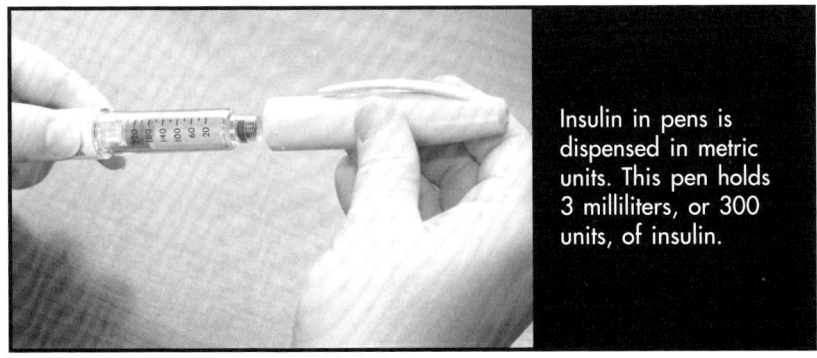

Insulin in pens is dispensed in metric units. This pen holds 3 milliliters, or 300 units, of insulin.

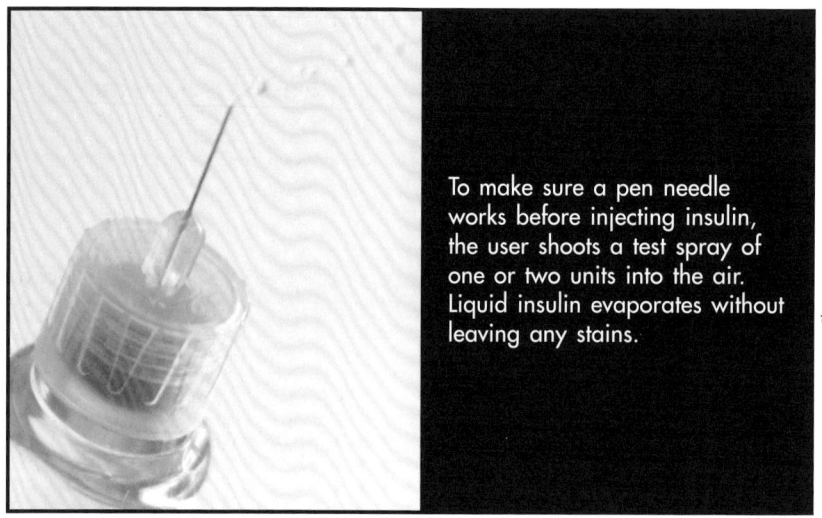

To make sure a pen needle works before injecting insulin, the user shoots a test spray of one or two units into the air. Liquid insulin evaporates without leaving any stains.

injecting the insulin. Pens store easily and require fewer supplies. Jet injectors shoot insulin through the skin with high-pressure air rather than a needle. This method is expensive and can be painful.

Insulin works best when injected into fatty tissue under the skin. From there, the insulin goes directly into the bloodstream. The abdomen provides the most effective place to distribute insulin evenly. But many people find it easier to inject insulin into their hips, thighs, or upper arms.

Another delivery method is the *insulin pump*, a pager-sized electronic device worn outside the body on a belt or inside a pocket. The pump delivers a small, steady flow of insulin throughout the day. Insulin goes through a flexible plastic tube inserted under the skin, usually in the abdomen. Insulin pumps can be programmed to deliver varying amounts of glucose into the system. Programming provides better blood sugar control by allowing users to customize their insulin delivery based on changes, such as physical activity, meals, and illness.

Newer models of pumps combine insulin delivery with a glucose meter. Parents of children with diabetes often prefer using a pump because they can give insulin without repeated injections. Pumps allow for a more "normal" lifestyle, but they cost more than pens, need additional supplies, and may require more attention.

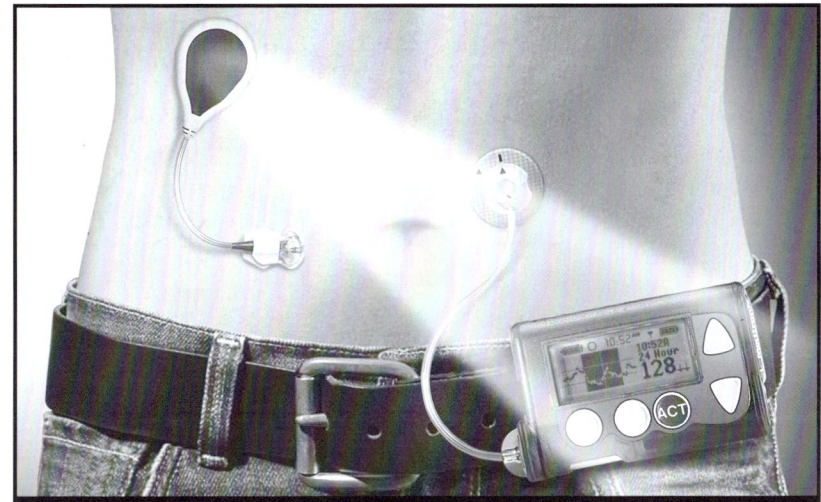

A model shows how a combination of a continuous glucose monitor *(left)* and insulin pump *(right)* may be worn attached to the abdomen. The device on the belt controls both the monitor and the pump. It also saves blood sugar data, which may be downloaded to a computer for closer examination.

An inhaled form of insulin became available in 2006. Powdered insulin from a handheld inhaler goes directly into lungs, where it is absorbed in the bloodstream. Inhaled insulin eases the burden of frequent injections but replaces only rapid-acting injectable insulin. To date, inhaled insulin has been approved for use by adults only.

Chapter 6

# PROBLEMS OF UNCONTROLLED DIABETES

## Abby's Story

*Eighteen-year-old Abby liked to pretend that she did not have type 1 diabetes. She told only her closest friends she had the condition. She rarely tested her blood sugar in front of anyone. She took insulin and tested her blood sugar at bedtime, but she wasn't doing everything she could to keep her diabetes under control.*

*For Abby, having diabetes wasn't cool—but being thin was. She received positive attention for losing weight. Her weight loss was not a good sign, however. It meant that her sugar levels were unstable. She became dehydrated because too much water left her body. Her lips and tongue always seemed dry. She often felt tired and out of sorts. Although friends thought Abby looked great, she was getting sicker.*

*One day after basketball practice, Abby seemed confused. Her speech was slurred. Since she had not told anyone about her diabetes, her teammates and coach didn't know what was wrong. Then Abby fainted, and the coach called an ambulance. The paramedics determined that Abby had hypoglycemia. They revived her with a shot of* glucagon, *a hormone that prompts the liver to convert glycogen into glucose and release it into the bloodstream. At the hospital, Abby was admitted so doctors and hospital staff could help her plan how to better control her diabetes.*

Even when treatment generally works to keep blood glucose levels within a stable range, dangerous problems can occur. Illness, a change in diet or activity, or another incident can throw blood sugars off kilter. Hypoglycemia or

## FACTORS THAT AFFECT BLOOD SUGAR LEVELS

Anything that puts stress on the body can affect blood sugar regulation and the body's use of glucose. Glucose levels may change in response to many factors, including:

- Food amounts, choices, and meal and snack times
- Exercise
- Alcoholic beverages
- Hormone changes
- Illness
- Stress
- Medications
- Amount of sleep

hyperglycemia may result. A third short-term problem from unstable blood sugar levels is the release of toxic acids into the blood and urine (*ketoacidosis*). Any of these extreme situations signals that the body is in trouble and requires immediate attention.

## HYPOGLYCEMIA: LOW BLOOD SUGAR

Blood sugar levels that plunge too low (hypoglycemia) can trigger sudden sweating and feelings of being jittery, drained, confused, or extremely hungry. As glucose levels drop lower, hearing problems, blurred vision, and headache may occur. If left untreated, low blood sugar can cause loss of consciousness or coma.

Another name for hypoglycemia is "insulin reaction." The name reflects the drop in blood sugar levels in response

## EMERGENCY IDENTIFICATION

High or low blood sugars increase the risk of a serious medical emergency. Problems can develop quickly and among strangers. In some instances, a person having a diabetic reaction may look weird, drunk, or scary. To alert others about what is happening, people with diabetes wear a medical identification bracelet or necklace. These tell strangers that the wearer has diabetes and provide emergency numbers to contact. Paramedics are trained to check the wrist and the neck for this life-saving jewelry.

"I wear a medical alert bracelet, and many people ask about it," Emily says. "I think it's important that people I spend a lot of time with know in case something happens."

to too much insulin in the system. Hypoglycemia may result from taking too much insulin, eating too little food, being sick, exercising, or drinking alcohol. Falling sugar levels are dangerous because the nervous system relies on glucose to work correctly.

"Low blood sugars. Those are the worst," Jared says. "I like to think of it as you drop a notch on the evolutionary totem pole. Your brain doesn't work. Sometimes you can't even help yourself. All of a sudden it takes effort just to reach for a Coke."

Hypoglycemia can be treated easily by eating or drinking something that contains sugar, such as fruit juice or an orange. Problems from occasional low blood sugar usually cause no permanent damage.

Diabetes educators suggest that people with diabetes always carry snacks with them in case of emergency. Sugar-containing snacks include hard candies, fruit juice, skim milk, raisins, or sugar cubes. Chewable glucose tablets, sold at drugstores, also provide a quick surge of sugar and are easy to carry.

## HYPERGLYCEMIA: HIGH BLOOD SUGAR

Signs of hyperglycemia include extreme thirst, frequent urination, blurred vision, vomiting, and unexplained weight loss. Left untreated, hyperglycemia can lead to weakness, confusion, *dehydration*, and cool hands and feet. Over time, hyperglycemia damages small and large blood vessels.

Illness, hormone changes, and stress can trigger hyperglycemia. So can drinking alcoholic beverages, eating too much, and inactivity.

## KETOACIDOSIS: INCREASED BLOOD ACIDS

When Jared first learned he had diabetes, he hardly realized anything was wrong. Gradually, he learned the warning signs, including frequent bathroom trips, thirst, and a different taste in his mouth. "Your saliva has different compounds that taste sour," Jared notes. "You can feel your salivary glands produce this sour taste."

The compounds Jared noticed are called *ketones*. These are toxic fatty acids that are produced when the body breaks down fat. When too little insulin is available to allow cells to receive glucose, the body turns to fat for fuel. As a result, ketones are released into the bloodstream and urine. Increased acids produce the bitterness that Jared tastes when his sugar levels rise. This condition is called diabetic ketoacidosis (DKA).

Ketoacidosis usually occurs when diabetes is undiagnosed, untreated, or uncontrolled. Illness, stress, or missing an insulin shot can stimulate acid buildup as well. Ketoacidosis is more common among people with type 1 diabetes, but it can happen with type 2 too. Some warning signs are the same as for diabetes: dry mouth and frequent urination. Other signs appear more flulike, including:

- stomach pain
- bouts of nausea or flushed skin
- sour, fruity breath
- fever or flushed skin
- rapid breathing
- loss of appetite
- weakness
- sleepiness

If you experience these symptoms, test your blood sugar level. Doctors recommend testing urine for ketones, since excess acid spills into urine. Chemically treated test strips change color when dipped into urine. The strips show whether ketone levels are low, medium, or high by changing color. You can also buy a meter to test blood ketones at home, which provides more accurate results than strips.

Ketoacidosis requires immediate medical attention. Insulin injections usually bring sugar and ketone levels back to normal. But you may also need large amounts of fluids to replace lost liquid and nutrients. Without immediate care, ketoacidosis can lead to loss of consciousness and death. With prompt treatment, however, symptoms usually disappear completely.

## HEART AND BLOOD VESSEL DISEASE

Cardiovascular disease—disease of the heart and blood vessels—is the major cause of death among people with diabetes. Diabetes interferes with how blood circulates through the body. Sugar buildup in the blood thickens and slows its flow through small and large blood vessels. With reduced blood flow, less glucose, oxygen, and other nutrients reach cells. Without these substances, cells become injured or die.

Cell death from elevated blood sugar damages *arteries*, the large vessels that carry blood from the heart to body tissues and organs. The damage makes it easier for fatty deposits (plaque) to form in the arteries, clogging or narrowing them. Too much fat in the bloodstream drives up blood pressure—the force of blood against artery walls. High blood pressure contributes to heart disease. People with diabetes are two to four times more likely than people without the illness to develop heart disease. Their risk of stroke, when a blood vessel in the brain is blocked or leaks, increases fivefold.

## NERVE DAMAGE

The nervous system contains a large network of nerves that carry messages between the brain and other body parts. High levels of glucose can damage nerves anywhere in the system. When damage occurs, messages may slow, send the wrong signal, or stop transmitting altogether.

Nerve damage, called *neuropathy*, contributes to a wide range of problems, depending on which nerves are affected. For example, decreased communication to body organs can disturb digestion, breathing, bladder and bowel function, and sexual performance. Neuropathy can cause pain, numbness, and tingling in feet, arms, and hands, and loss of balance. Without feeling, these areas are more prone to bruising and infection. Someone who does not feel pain might not notice a cut or wound. As the infection spreads, cells in the limb can die. In some cases, the limb must be amputated (surgically removed).

## EYE DAMAGE

Tiny blood vessels nourish the back part of the eye, called the retina. The retina senses light to produce images. High blood sugar damages eye blood vessels, interfering with incoming light. Problems in the retina are referred to as *retinopathy*.

Eye damage worsens the longer diabetes remains untreated or uncontrolled. As blood becomes thick with sugar, vessels in the retina swell or bulge. Weakened, swollen blood vessels can leak blood into the eye, reducing vision more. In some cases, new blood vessels form. These vessels are weak and spread wildly, further interfering with vision.

Eye damage eventually affects almost all people with type 1 diabetes and more than six out of ten with type 2. Poorly controlled diabetes is the leading cause of blindness in U.S. adults under the age of sixty-five. People with diabetes can lower their risk of retinopathy and other diabetes-related eye problems by keeping glucose levels within a normal range and having a yearly eye exam. Eye doctors can detect signs of eye disease

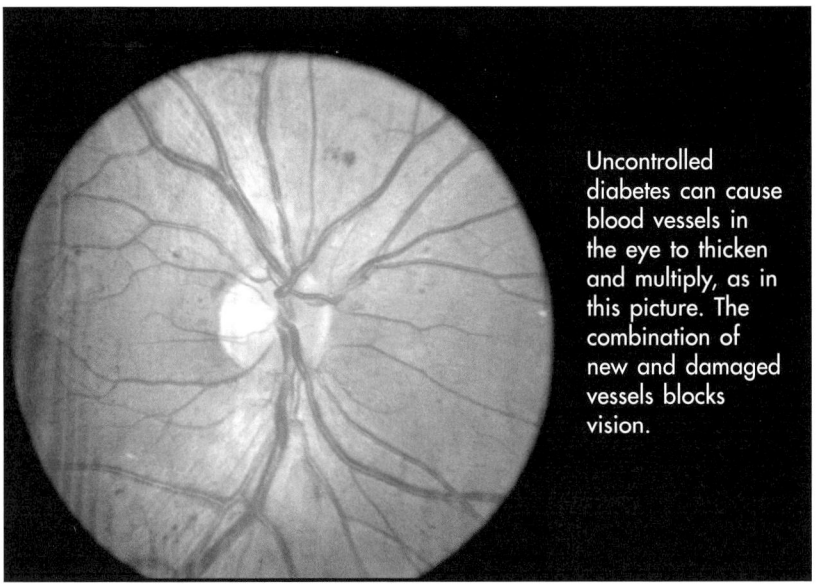

Uncontrolled diabetes can cause blood vessels in the eye to thicken and multiply, as in this picture. The combination of new and damaged vessels blocks vision.

before patients notice symptoms. Treatment usually stops eye damage from progressing if caught early.

## KIDNEY DISEASE

Diabetes interferes with the kidneys' normal filtering system. Your two kidneys sit in back of your abdomen on both sides of the spine and just below the waist. Their job is to receive oxygen-rich blood from the heart, remove waste products from the blood, and discharge waste in urine. Kidney disease, or *nephropathy*, can develop when blood sugar levels remain elevated over a period of time.

Studies indicate that kidney changes occur within three years of high glucose levels. Sugar damages the tiny blood vessels that strain waste from the blood. Therefore, waste products remain in the system, crowding out nutrients and causing other problems.

Symptoms of kidney damage include swollen feet, ankles, and hands, and fatigue. If untreated, nephropathy can lead to difficulty concentrating, nausea and vomiting, loss of appetite, high blood pressure, and eventually kidney failure. According to the American Diabetes Association, "Kidneys have so much extra filtering ability that noticeable problems will not appear until 80 percent of the kidneys are damaged."

Urine tests can pick up early signs of kidney disease, though. So if you have diabetes, regular exams are important. Keeping blood sugar under control can reduce the risk of kidney problems. Lowering high blood pressure reduces stress on the kidneys' delicate blood vessels. Maintaining a healthy weight is one way to lower blood pressure. Another is to reduce the amount of salt, or sodium, in your diet.

The longer someone has diabetes, the greater the threat of getting kidney disease. Three in ten people with type 1 and one in ten with type 2 diabetes eventually experience some form of kidney disease. Diabetes is the primary cause of kidney failure in the United States.

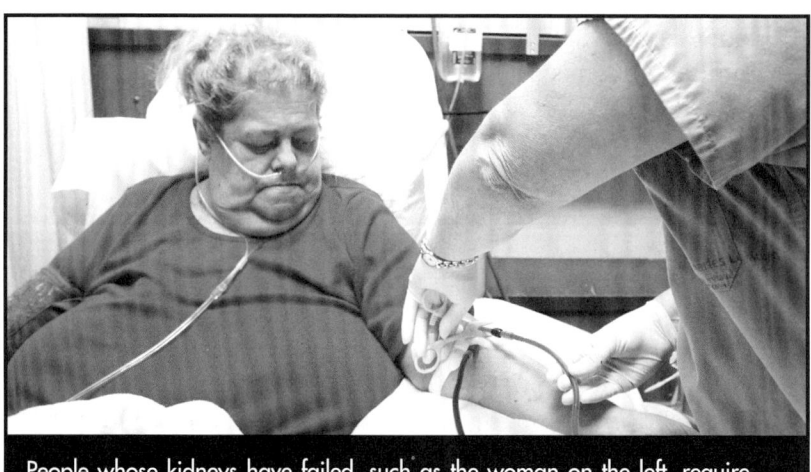

People whose kidneys have failed, such as the woman on the left, require about three sessions on a dialysis machine each week. In three to five hours per session, dialysis cleans their blood.

## MEMORY LOSS

Recent studies link diabetes with *Alzheimer's disease*, which damages the brain and causes memory loss. According to these studies, people with type 2 diabetes are twice as likely to develop Alzheimer's disease as people without diabetes. Scientists believe that circulation problems caused by diabetes interfere with blood flow to the brain, damaging brain cells that contribute to memory.

Researchers are investigating a destructive protein called *amyloid*, which is involved in both Alzheimer's disease and diabetes. When amyloid clumps together, it forms gooey plaques in the brain, causing memory problems seen in Alzheimer's disease. In people with type 2 diabetes, amyloid builds up in the pancreas. But too much insulin in the brain—caused when cells resist insulin—can lead to amyloid buildup in the brain.

## INFECTIONS

People with uncontrolled diabetes experience more infections than the average person. High blood sugar levels hamper the immune system's ability to destroy germs that attack the body. People with diabetes face a greater risk of infection in the skin, feet, gums, and vagina. Once germs enter the body, they feed on extra sugar in the blood. Without treatment, infections can lead to more serious problems. Diabetes educators advise patients to brush and floss regularly to reduce the threat of gum disease, check their feet daily for cuts or other wounds, and stay alert to even the most minor injury.

New research indicates that temperature may help people without feeling in their feet detect possible infections. A rise in body temperature can signal infection. One doctor found that the same is true for the bottom of feet. He encourages his patients with diabetes to keep track of the temperature of their feet using an infrared thermometer. If either foot varies in temperature, the patient should stay off the warmer foot and see the doctor. The doctor believes that this simple technique prevents sores and more serious problems from developing.

## PREVENTING PROBLEMS

Learning about everything that can go wrong if you have diabetes can be scary. But a diagnosis of diabetes does not automatically mean that you'll get complications. Many factors play a role in how the disease develops. Anyone with diabetes can take steps to manage the disease and help prevent complications:

- Keep tight control of glucose levels, and follow your treatment plan.
- Schedule a yearly physical exam and appointments with the eye doctor, foot doctor, and dentist.
- See your diabetes doctor for regular checkups.
- Brush and floss your teeth twice a day.
- Stay up to date with vaccinations for flu and other illnesses.
- Take good care of your feet.
- Don't smoke.
- Avoid alcohol.
- Find healthy ways to relieve stress. (*Check out the tips in the next chapter.*)

*Chapter 7*

# ADJUSTING TO LIFE WITH DIABETES

## Brianna's Story

*Twenty-year-old Brianna discovered she had type 1 diabetes when she was fifteen. Her older sister had been diagnosed at the age of twelve, so the family recognized the symptoms. After Brianna was diagnosed, she attended classes at a local hospital to learn how to inject insulin and balance her food intake. After a few weeks, following her diabetes treatment plan came naturally to her. She found it fairly easy to control her glucose levels, and most of the time, she didn't think about her disease.*

*But after her last doctor's appointment, Brianna realized that she didn't want to have diabetes anymore. Maybe it was the constant checking of blood sugar—in the morning, after meals, at bedtime. The routine was getting annoying and old.*

*Every time she went to the doctor, her care team discussed changes she needed to make to be healthier. This was probably true for everybody. But knowing that her diabetes was going to last forever was hard.*

## A LIFELONG ILLNESS

Medical professionals cannot offer a quick fix or cure for diabetes. People who have the condition must pay attention to their diet, activities, and other health issues all day, every day, their whole life. Losing weight, adjusting diet and medication, and monitoring glucose levels all take time and energy. Even under the best circumstances, managing diabetes can be difficult. But many people have found ways to make life with diabetes easier.

Understanding the ups and downs of having diabetes can be helpful. Everyone normally goes through periods of feeling sad, happy, or angry. A long-term disease adds extra challenges. The diabetes care team can help with understanding these reactions and offer tips for getting through tough periods. They have information about joining a support group, where people with diabetes share their emotional journey and offer suggestions for making life with a long-term illness easier.

## MIXED FEELINGS

When you first learn you have diabetes, you may feel overwhelmed, afraid, worried, sad, or angry. These are all common reactions. Over time, your feelings may seesaw. Unexpected problems may spark disappointment or embarrassment about having a body that does not work properly.

One in five people with diabetes experiences depression—a deep sadness or sense of hopelessness that continues for weeks or months. People who are depressed no longer find joy in everyday activities. They may lack energy to care for their diabetes. Sadness that lasts more than two weeks for no apparent reason requires professional help. Counseling or psychotherapy, support groups, medication, or a combination of these treatments can help ease depression.

Everyone with diabetes handles the challenges differently. Some people deny they have the disease. They keep it a secret from friends, teachers, and coworkers. Other people talk openly about the condition and feel comfortable testing their blood sugar and injecting insulin in public.

## SUPPORTING A FRIEND WITH DIABETES

If your friend, family member, or other loved one has diabetes, here are some ways you can help them.

**Do:**
- Treat your friend normally.
- Ask your friend what signs point to trouble.
- Ask what you should do in case of trouble.
- Stay with a friend in trouble.
- Tell your friend something positive each day.

**Don't:**
- Nag.
- Tell friends with diabetes what they can and cannot do, unless you see risky behavior.
- Monitor what your friend eats or drinks.
- Tempt or pressure your friend to eat or drink anything he or she turns down.
- Blame a friend for highs and lows.

"Diabetes is an invasion of the body and sense of self," says Melissa, a social worker who has had diabetes since childhood. "I think it's made me look toward the future more than I would otherwise. Diabetes can also make you worry a lot. I might obsess about having diabetes but not do enough. Other people get very compulsive, testing and watching everything they eat and do."

A few people focus on their disease to an unhealthy extreme. They dwell on diabetes to the point that it interferes with relationships, leisure activities, and a balanced lifestyle. With time, however, most people learn to accept and live with the condition.

### CHILDREN WITH DIABETES

Diabetes is a family affair, especially when children have the disease. Life changes for everyone in the household. A diabetes treatment plan may require particular snacks, mealtimes, and planned activities. Creating a balance between diabetes planning and everyday activities helps ease the stress that diabetes can place on families.

## DIABETES CAMP

Children with diabetes can attend camps just for kids like them. Diabetes camps tailor meals to individual food plans and hire on-staff medical teams with diabetes experience. At these special camps, kids can have fun while getting to know other children with diabetes. Camps are located throughout the United States. Families can locate a camp at www.childrenwithdiabetes.com/camps or through the American Diabetes Association.

Parents of young children with diabetes must manage the disease and help their child cope with it. The parents' tasks include staying alert to symptoms, monitoring blood sugar, injecting insulin, and preparing foods according to plan. Diabetes requires parents to plan ahead for situations, such as birthday parties, sleepovers, camp, trick-or-treating, and anything else that could be a trouble spot. Parents may prepare healthy snacks to send with their child to a party or sleepover. They might host a Halloween party at home, where they can control the treats and give presents instead of candy to trick-or-treaters.

Diabetes in the home can become overwhelming at times. Parents often blame themselves for their child's condition. They worry that they fed their child the wrong foods or passed on a family disease. Brothers and sisters may feel that the child with diabetes gets special attention for being sick. Families need to strike a balance between managing the disease and addressing each family member's needs.

"In a way, it was like having an infant again," remembers Jared's mother, Ann. "The condition was a lot to get used to."

## DIABETES AND SCHOOL

Going to school presents special challenges for children with diabetes. They need to eat more frequently to keep blood sugar levels stable. They may not be able to eat the same foods as their classmates at lunchtime or for snacks. Children with diabetes may encounter discrimination or unfair treatment from people who know little about their disease. Some teachers cannot understand why a child needs to leave the room or have food in class. Classmates might tease or bully someone they view as different. Situations like these can make a child feel different.

Parents find it helpful to work closely with teachers and principals to come up with strategies that work, even if it means bending some school rules. Students with diabetes must be allowed to eat in class, stop physical activity if necessary, and leave the classroom to visit the school nurse or test blood sugar. Since children spend so much time in school, teachers play an important role in helping students with diabetes stay healthy. But parents should alert bus drivers, librarians, lunchroom attendants, and other school personnel who come in contact with their child as well.

"The school nurse and I talked every day about how Jared was doing," Ann remembers. "The nurse checked his blood sugar every day."

Some parents and children make a presentation about diabetes to the class to let other students know more about diabetes. Classmates learn they cannot catch diabetes and what treatment involves. Knowing about a condition reduces fear, teasing, and bullying. Equally important, classmates and teachers learn that people with diabetes are more than their illness. They learn about someone who is just like them, with the same range of abilities, interests, and hopes.

If teachers or school administrators resist making accommodations for a child with diabetes, parents have resources to help. Disability laws guarantee all children the right to an education. (See "Resources" on page 106 for organizations that assist families dealing with disability or illness.)

## TEENS WITH DIABETES

"Doctors suggest testing blood sugar before a meal," says Melissa. "You tell me how many teens are going to want to do this when they are out with friends or alone. Teenagers—and adults—don't always know what they're going to eat during a meal. They can't plan appropriately. I still have to force myself, and I'm an adult."

Teenage years can be complicated even if you don't have diabetes. If you do, the illness adds other layers of

## DIABETES AND SMOKING

Diabetes and smoking don't mix. Smoking reduces the amount of oxygen reaching body tissues and raises blood sugar levels. These factors make maintaining good diabetes control more difficult. Smoking and diabetes contribute to a higher risk of infection, heart disease, stroke, nerve damage, and birth defects. Cutting back on smoking helps reduce some of the negative effects. But it's best to stop smoking altogether or never start, especially if you have diabetes.

complexity. On the physical level, hormonal changes can affect diabetes control and insulin resistance. On the emotional level, diabetes may create tension between parents and children. Teens want to be independent. They like to experiment and act spontaneously. These natural longings can interfere with tight control of their diabetes. Parents may find letting go difficult because they worry about their teen's health.

Teens with diabetes may feel deprived and frustrated. They rebel by eating the wrong foods, not getting enough sleep, or drinking alcohol. They might refuse to test their blood sugar or take their insulin. But sooner or later, these behaviors catch up with them, leading to health problems.

With time, however, many teens figure out how to keep themselves safe and still have fun. For example, if blood sugar levels drop, alert teens let someone else drive the car or they sit out during part of a sports game. They remember to bring healthy snacks whenever they go out. They reach out to friends who will support them.

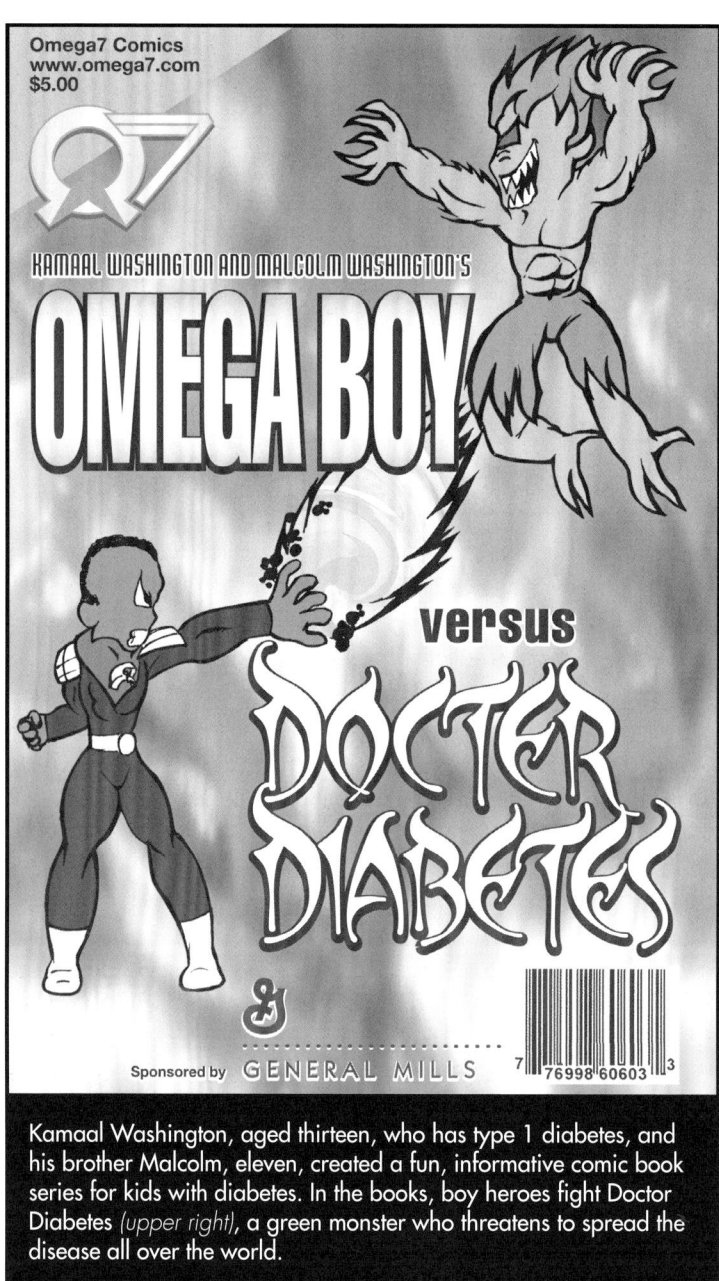

Kamaal Washington, aged thirteen, who has type 1 diabetes, and his brother Malcolm, eleven, created a fun, informative comic book series for kids with diabetes. In the books, boy heroes fight Doctor Diabetes *(upper right)*, a green monster who threatens to spread the disease all over the world.

Preteens and teens with diabetes have a big homework assignment. They must learn to manage the chronic disease on their own.

"I think I've always been lucky in that most of my friends are just interested in knowing about diabetes," Emily says. "I believe they look out for me. In high school, my friends made sure I ate enough at lunch. If I had low blood sugar, they walked with me to the nurse's office. In college, my friends joined my family in a fund-raising diabetes walk. My brother and I don't hide diabetes in public, although I might be a bit more careful about whipping out needles with a new date. From time to time someone is grossed out by needles, and it's understandable. In general, everyone is very supportive and helpful."

## REDUCING STRESS

"Diabetes is an inconvenience," Carl, who has type 2 diabetes, says. "I take my insulin supplies everywhere and plan before I go. It looks like I'm carrying a purse around with me. Before meals at restaurants, I have to excuse myself to go to the bathroom and check my glucose level or inject insulin. When I have low blood sugar, I get light-headed. Sometimes when I delay taking insulin, I have low-grade pain throughout my body. It means sugar is stealing energy from my body cells. I have my challenges, but I'm happy to deal with them. The alternative is much worse."

Repeatedly squeezing a spongy stress ball is a handy stress management technique.

Having a chronic illness is stressful. Following daily insulin routines, managing blood sugar levels, and dealing with pain can take a toll on the most laid-back person. And stress affects blood sugar levels, creating a downward spiral. Hormones in the body that respond to stress alter body chemistry, causing blood sugar levels to spike or plunge. These stress hormones can increase insulin resistance and raise blood pressure.

Managing stress is critical to overall health for people with diabetes. One study found that people with type 2 diabetes who included stress management techniques in their routine care significantly reduced their average blood glucose levels. But eliminating stress entirely is unrealistic. Some stress is part of everyday life for everyone. Instead, doctors counsel people with diabetes to look for ways to reduce stresses in their lives and better manage what comes their way.

"There are conditions in our life that are chronic; they're not going to go away; they just can't be fixed; and the real way of managing that is to come to terms on the inside with ourselves, with our own reactions to whatever the world is giving us," says Dr. Jeffrey Brantley of Duke University Medical Center.

Many different activities and techniques reduce stress. Exercise is one of the best because it helps with blood sugar and weight control. "Exercise makes me feel better able to cope with life," says Jared. The following additional strategies help people with diabetes manage stress and stay healthy.

**Planning Ahead**

This sounds simple, but how many people really plan ahead? Most fly out the door two seconds before a bus is due, or they grab an apple on the way out the door in the morning. Yet preparing for situations before they happen reduces stress.

For people with diabetes, planning ahead becomes even more important. This means knowing what to do in case of low or high blood sugars and having the correct supplies on hand. Planning ahead involves working with your care team to create a written treatment program that includes actions to follow during medical emergencies.

The American Diabetes Association recommends keeping a packed emergency kit. The kit should contain diabetes supplies for three days, including medications

A nurse reviews the diabetes supplies that a young person needs in his first aid kit.

and insulin, quick-acting glucose tablets, snacks, injection supplies, testing materials, and batteries for meters, monitors, or pumps. The kit should also identify emergency contacts, doctor's orders, and names of school staff or coworkers who can help.

Planning ahead involves preparing for situations that could interfere with following a normal diet, testing blood sugar, or taking insulin. For example, before going to a party or off for a day at the beach, consider what snacks to take, where and when to test blood sugar, and where to inject insulin privately, if this is a concern. Other situations that require planning ahead include travel, holidays, dates, and other special events.

**Support Groups**

Many people with diabetes and their family members find support groups helpful. Regular group meetings provide a place to talk about diabetes with people who understand what living with the disease is like. A support group offers a relaxed setting where members feel accepted and understood. Group members share tips and information and offer suggestions for dealing with diabetes.

Support groups are available for people of all ages and for family members who need a place to talk about their spouse, child, or parent with diabetes. The American Diabetes Association provides information about where to find support groups in your area.

**Relaxation Techniques**

A variety of relaxation techniques can help relieve stress. Simple ways of relaxing include listening to music and deep breathing. Anyone can do these activities without special training or expense.

Another easy method to reduce stress involves progressive muscle relaxation. With this activity, you sit or lie in a comfortable position. Then focus on tightening and loosening muscles in each body part, one at a time.

Some people find stress relief through *visualization*, a relaxation technique in which you picture, or visualize, a peaceful or healthy situation. For example, you could picture yourself jogging without a sugar low, or watching a sunset or ocean waves lapping on a sandy beach. By creating an image of your body in a relaxed, balanced, and healthy state, you reinforce the message that your body is strong and can heal itself. People who practice visualization regularly report the technique helps them maintain a sense of calm and well-being. In turn, the calm helps control diabetes by reducing blood pressure and diabetes-related pain.

What kind of scene would you visualize to help yourself relax? You can travel anywhere your imagination takes you.

Many people find *meditation* produces similar results. With meditation, you focus on your breathing or on a single word or object to reach a relaxed, focused mental state. Studies show that meditation can reduce muscle tension, slow pulse rate, and lower blood pressure.

Yoga is a simple way to relax through deep concentration and a variety of specific body positions.

Yoga provides many of the same benefits. Yoga exercises combine deep breathing with physical poses that stretch muscles. Over time, yoga exercises build considerable muscle strength and flexibility. Because these exercises require physical and mental control, they increase the capacity for exercise, which eases stress on the body during activity.

## BIOFEEDBACK

*Biofeedback* teaches people to become aware of their body's automatic and unconscious processes, such as heart rate and skin temperature. This awareness helps them gain control over the processes. To begin biofeedback, a trained practitioner connects the patient to a machine that records a specific body function, such as heart rate. The machine relays information about the body's responses as sounds, numbers on a screen, or other visual cues. Gradually, the mind learns to connect these responses with body changes.

Therapists sometimes use biofeedback with other relaxation techniques, such as visualization, to enhance self-awareness. For example, when a biofeedback signal indicates muscle tightening, the patient becomes better able to isolate the problem and use muscle relaxation or another technique to lessen discomfort.

## ACUPUNCTURE

*Acupuncture* is widely practiced in China, where the technique began more than five thousand years ago. According to Chinese medicine, a life force known as chi flows like a river through several pathways in the body. As chi circulates, it cleanses and nourishes tissues in different organs. The free flow of chi ensures good health. But an imbalance of chi or a blocked pathway signals ill health, much as a dam backs up a river's flow.

Acupuncture seeks to unblock the dam and correct chi imbalances to restore health. The main focus of acupuncture treatment for diabetes is to relieve chronic pain, such as from nerve damage. Trained acupuncture practitioners insert thin needles at specific points along the pathways. Needles are thought to stimulate the release of the body's natural painkillers. The patient feels less pain, which reduces stress.

Chapter 8

# DARK HISTORY, BRIGHTER FUTURE

## Jamie's Story

*Jamie, aged seven, was born with type 1 diabetes. Her parents first learned that their daughter had diabetes when she was one month old. From then on, the family checked Jamie's blood sugar levels and injected insulin several times a day. Jamie endured constant finger sticks and food monitoring.*

*This routine lasted for six years. Jamie's world changed after her father heard a doctor talk about a study of children diagnosed with diabetes before six months of age. Researchers at Peninsula Medical School in the United Kingdom found that some newborns showed changes in one of two key genes involving insulin-producing beta cells. If Jamie was one of those rare children, her diabetes might respond to medication.*

*Jamie's saliva was tested for the genetic changes, and results showed a match. Her altered genes reduced her body's ability to produce insulin. This finding turned out to be wonderful news. Jamie's form of diabetes responded to the sulfonylurea class of drugs normally used for type 2 diabetes. After a week on this medication, Jamie's body produced insulin for the first time. She still needed to watch what she ate and get her blood tested. But she took pills and her parents tested her blood sugar only twice a day to regulate glucose levels. She no longer needed insulin injections.*

## SEARCHING FOR A CURE

Research into diabetes continually expands what is known about the disease. New discoveries change how people with diabetes live and how long they can live without problems related to the disease. But this was not always the case. At one time, high blood sugar meant certain death, as people with diabetes became dehydrated and wasted away. Over the centuries, doctors tried various treatments to keep people from dying of diabetes. During the 1700s and 1800s, doctors cut patients' veins to allow blood to drip out in a process known as bloodletting.

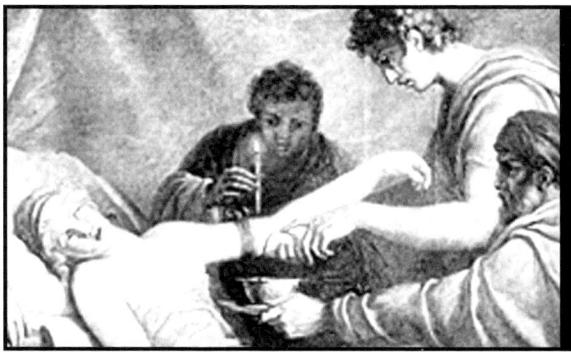

Making a person bleed sounds contrary to improving health. Yet bloodletting was common practice to treat most diseases, including diabetes, until the 1800s.

Doctors gave patients substances to make them vomit or to clean out their bowels. Some doctors wrapped patients in warm flannel or rubbed them down with a brush or coarse towel to make them sweat. When these procedures failed, doctors prescribed strong drugs, such as morphine or opium. None of these treatments reduced the dire effects of diabetes.

During the late 1800s, diabetes treatment began to include restricted diets. One program required fasting for several days followed by a limited diet. The meal plan consisted of "plain blood puddings" that mixed fat, blood, and spoiled meat. Other diets permitted only green vegetables or oatmeal, rice, potatoes, or milk. But these diets failed to save patients.

## THE DISCOVERY OF INSULIN

In 1889 German scientists Joseph von Mering and Oskar Minkowski conducted a breakthrough experiment. While investigating digestion of fats, they removed a dog's pancreas. Their experiment yielded unexpected results. Within a short time, the dog began to urinate often. And the men noticed the urine attracted swarms of flies. Curious, the two tested the urine and discovered that it contained a large amount of sugar. Von Mering and Minkowski concluded that substances produced in the pancreas must control sugar levels in the body. This finding linked the pancreas to diabetes.

Many researchers tried to figure out how the pancreas controlled blood sugar. In 1921 a young Canadian doctor, Frederick Banting, and his assistant, Charles Best, removed a dog's pancreas and extracted a substance from the islets of Langerhans. These cells were named for Paul Langerhans, the scientist who had first described them in 1869. Banting then put the extract back into the dog's bloodstream. The injection resulted in blood sugar levels returning to normal and sugar-free urine.

Experimentation on animals was more socially acceptable in the early 1900s. Scientists Charles Best *(left)* and Frederick Banting pose here with the first dog to be kept alive by insulin.

Banting worked under the supervision of Professor John Macleod, who was thrilled with the results. Macleod thought the extract was a hormone, which he named insulin. Macleod encouraged Banting to perform more studies. After several successful trials with dogs, Banting experimented with using insulin in humans with diabetes. For these patients, he collected insulin from cow pancreases.

Banting's first injection into a fourteen-year-old boy with diabetes showed little promise. Macleod worked with biochemist J. B. Collip on better ways to extract the hormone from cows and purify it for human use. The cleaner insulin achieved success. Within two weeks, the boy, who originally weighed only 65 pounds (29 kg), gained weight and looked stronger. He continued to thrive for the next fifteen years, as long as he received insulin injections.

News of this breakthrough treatment rocked the medical community. Within a year, large-scale production of insulin from cows and pigs began. Newspapers and professional journals heralded insulin as a cure for diabetes. In 1923 Banting and Mcleod received the Nobel Prize for the discovery and development of insulin. Banting shared his prize with Best, and Mcleod shared his with Collip.

## NEW HOPE

The discovery of insulin in 1921 brought new hope and the promise of longer lives for people with diabetes. But the ups and downs of managing insulin and diet continued to pose challenges. Doctors learned that diabetes affected more than just sugar levels: it damaged the heart, nervous system, kidneys, and eyes. Researchers continued to look for ways to refine treatment and reduce complications.

During the 1930s, chemists created a longer-acting form of insulin. About twenty years later, the first oral medications for people with type 2 diabetes became available. In 1958 Canadian physician Frederick Sanger separated cow insulin into its simplest components. His discovery paved the way for insulin to be chemically engineered, so that it mirrored what humans produce naturally. In recent years, several new drugs for diabetes have been developed.

Along with new forms of insulin and medications, manufacturers developed better needles, test strips, glucose meters, continuous glucose monitors and insulin pumps. Even with these advances, however, doctors continue to promote self-testing with a meter to verify the accuracy of other devices.

"Six years after I was diagnosed at age twelve, doctors came up with so much research," Melissa says. "When I was diagnosed, we were still doing urine testing to detect sugar. They did not have short-acting insulin. You could not test blood on your own. You had to go to a doctor. Mostly, the amount of control you could get changed so much."

## THE FUTURE

Medical science has come a long way toward understanding and treating diabetes. Still, the search for a cure is not over. Researchers continue to investigate advances that will make diabetes treatment easier and able to cure the disease completely.

### Breaking the Gene Code

In 2002 Boston scientists discovered a third gene related to

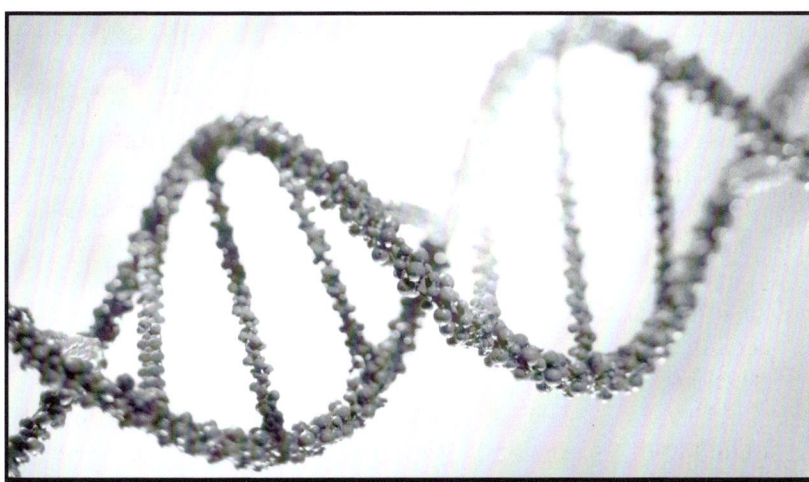

This model *(above)* represents a strand of deoxyribonucleic acid (DNA), the molecule in cells that carries an organism's genetic information. In the 1990s, the Human Genome Project completed a map of all the genes in human DNA. The project has led to discoveries about how specific genes contribute to diseases such as diabetes.

French researcher Philippe Froguel and scientists at Imperial College London identified the human genetic abnormality GAD2. It plays a role in the human body's healthy use of insulin. Further studies are under way to determine the gene's role in diabetes.

type 1 diabetes. They believe the three genes work as a team to control insulin production in beta cells. If any of these genes is faulty or missing, the pancreas cannot manufacture insulin. In 2007 researchers identified genes that predispose a person to develop type 2 diabetes. Scientists believe that these genes, located on three different chromosomes, explain much of the inherited tendency to acquire type 2 diabetes.

Understanding the genetics of diabetes can help scientists develop tests to screen for diabetes before it develops. This understanding may also help researchers develop new, healthy replacement genes from *stem cells*. Stem cells are unprogrammed cells that are capable of becoming any type of body cell. Most body cells carry codes that tell them to develop into a particular type of cell. But stem cells possess the ability to mature into any type of cell or organ, including beta cells in the pancreas. Stem cells hold great promise to replace damaged beta cells. Scientists are still working to understand how to program these cells into beta cells, however.

**Transplants**
Damaged organs may be replaced with healthy ones through transplant surgery. Some people with type 1 diabetes and severe complications have received a pancreas transplant. A healthy pancreas comes from a donor who has just died or a living relative who offers half his or her pancreas. The surgery poses risks for both patients, however, because any surgery is dangerous. What's more, the immune system in the person with diabetes may reject and attack the new pancreas. Transplant patients take medications to help curb rejection. But these drugs are costly, and they often cause other health problems.

Another type of transplant uses islet cells from a donor pancreas. Transplanting islet cells may help people with diabetes someday, but this surgery is still experimental and faces some of the same problems as pancreas transplants.

Researchers are investigating less dangerous antirejection medication and improved surgery techniques. One avenue of research explores a coating to protect transplanted islet cells from attack by the immune system. Another approach looks into creating artificial islet cells that can be implanted elsewhere in the body but will produce insulin whenever blood sugar levels rise.

**Immune Therapy**
In an effort to extend the honeymoon phase of type 1 diabetes and preserve the function of insulin-producing beta cells, researchers are using a technique called targeted

antibodies. These special antibodies latch onto a type of immune system cell that attacks beta cells in the pancreas. At first the patient's immune system cell counts drop. But when the antibodies multiply several weeks later, new immune system cells attack the beta cells in a different way. They seem reprogrammed. The effect might help preserve beta cell function for a year or longer. Research into this type of treatment is in an experimental phase.

**Implanted Monitors**
In addition to a cure, scientists are also investigating better ways to help patients control blood sugar levels. One goal is to "close the loop." This phrase refers to an all-in-one device that monitors blood sugar levels and automatically releases insulin when needed. Various versions of such devices have been developed already, but researchers are working to improve them. One version is surgically implanted in the body. Another stays outside the body but has a tube that goes through the skin. Both versions are being tested to see if they function as predicted and whether patients find them easier to use than those already on the market.

**Drug Prevention**
Diabetes is a complicated disease. And complications from uncontrolled blood sugar are expensive to manage and treat. That's why some drug manufacturers are concentrating on developing medications to prevent diabetes in millions of people at high risk for the disease. So far studies of one new drug indicated that people in this category reduced their chance of developing diabetes by two-thirds. But other tests of the same drug proved mixed, so government approval is a long way off.

Rising numbers of cases cause great concern for the health-care community. Government agencies, scientists, and manufacturers are investing time and money to find better ways to prevent and treat the disease. In the meantime, people with diabetes are learning more about how to help themselves.

"I try to plug diabetes into the natural way I think of the world," Jared explains. "You get what you put into what you do. If you're lazy and stupid about your care, you're going to have troubles. If you're vigilant, you'll have a successful life."

# GLOSSARY

**acupuncture:** an ancient medical practice that uses thin needles inserted along nerve pathways to relieve pain and treat disease

**Alzheimer's disease:** a brain disease characterized by protein plaques that interfere with transmission of messages, resulting in memory loss

**amyloid:** a destructive protein that may be involved in diabetes and Alzheimer's disease

**antibodies:** immune system units made of protein molecules that recognize, destroy, and remember invading microbes, such as bacteria and viruses

**arteries:** vessels that carry blood from the heart to all tissues and organs in the body

**autoantibodies:** immune system protein molecules that wrongly identify "foreign" substances and attack the body's own healthy cells

**autoimmune disease:** a disease that occurs when someone's immune system attacks his or her own tissues and cells

**beta cells:** cells in areas of the pancreas called islets. Beta cells make and release insulin, a hormone that controls the level of glucose (sugar) in the blood.

**biofeedback:** a technique to reduce stress and pain by learning to recognize and control changes in automatic body processes, such as heart rate

**blood glucose:** the amount of sugar (glucose) in the blood at a given time

**blood pressure:** the force of blood against artery walls. High blood pressure contributes to heart disease

**blood sugar:** an informal name for blood glucose

**blood sugar meter:** a device for testing how much glucose (sugar) is in the blood at one point in time

**carbohydrates:** one of the three major components of food, along with protein and fats. Carbohydrates supply the body's main source of energy.

**chromosomes:** rod-shaped structures within cells that contain genes, the basic units of heredity

**complex carbohydrates:** carbohydrates that come from sugars in whole-grain products, dried peas and beans, legumes, and starchy vegetables, such as potatoes and corn

**continuous glucose monitor (CGM):** a device made up of a sensor, which collects blood sugar readings from interstitial fluid, placed under the skin and a small monitor, which records the readings. Readings are taken approximately every five minutes, or 288 times every twenty-four hours.

**dehydration:** abnormal and excessive loss of body fluids

**diabetes:** a disease, also known as diabetes mellitus, that occurs when the body is unable to use sugar properly, resulting in high levels of blood sugar

**dieticians:** nutrition specialists who help plan healthy food choices and meals. A registered dietitian (R.D.) has special training.

**digestion:** the process whereby the body breaks down food into smaller particles to be used for fuel and nutrition

**endocrinologist:** a medical doctor trained to diagnose and treat disorders of the endocrine system

**endocrine system:** the glands and organs that produce hormones and release them into the bloodstream to help operate body processes, including metabolism (use of food for energy), growth, and sexual function

**fasting plasma glucose test:** a test for diabetes that measures glucose levels in blood plasma after a person has fasted (not eaten) for eight hours

**fiber:** a substance found in foods that come from plants, including whole-grain products, fruits, and vegetables

**genes:** chemical units in cells that contain coded instructions for forming proteins. Genes determine traits that are passed from parent to child.

**gestational diabetes:** a form of diabetes that develops during pregnancy

**glucagon:** a hormone that prompts the liver to convert glycogen into glucose and release it into the bloodstream. An injection of glucagon is used to revive someone who has lost consciousness due to hypoglycemia.

**glucose:** a type of sugar that the body makes from the elements of food—proteins, fats, and carbohydrates. Glucose comes mostly from carbohydrates and is the main source of fuel for growth and activity. Glucose cannot enter body cells without the help of insulin, which acts as a key or gatekeeper.

**glucose tolerance test:** a test for diabetes that shows blood sugar levels over time after a person drinks a sugary liquid

**glycogen:** sugar stored in the liver that is released when blood sugar levels drop too low and the body needs energy

**hormones:** chemicals produced in cells that travel in body fluids and stimulate other cells to do their job

**hyperglycemia:** high blood sugar

**hypoglycemia:** low blood sugar

**immune system:** the units of the body that work together to fight disease

**injections:** the use of a needle and syringe or pen to put liquid into the body

**insulin:** a hormone produced in the pancreas that acts as a gatekeeper to allow sugar to pass into cells

**insulin pump:** a device that delivers a continuous supply of rapid-acting insulin into the body through a thin, flexible plastic tube that is inserted into the skin

**insulin resistance:** a condition common in people with type 2 diabetes in which the body does not respond to insulin

**interstitial fluid:** clear fluid under the skin that carries glucose and other nutrients from the bloodstream to the cells

**islets:** clumps, or islands, of cells, also known as islets of Langerhans, found in the pancreas. Islets hold beta cells, which produce insulin.

**ketoacidosis:** severe, life-threatening disorder, also called diabetic ketoacidosis (DKA), caused by a lack of circulating insulin. The body uses stored fat for fuel, which results in production of toxic fatty acids called ketones.

**ketones:** fatty acids produced from the breakdown of fat for fuel

**lancet:** a sharp, fine needle that pricks the skin to draw blood for glucose testing

**meditation:** a form of relaxation that involves focusing on the breath, a word, or an object

**metabolism:** the way the body chemically changes food into the nutrients and energy needed to sustain life

**nephropathy:** kidney disease

**neuropathy:** nerve damage

**pancreas:** a small organ that lies behind the lower part of the stomach. As part of the endocrine system, the pancreas makes insulin and digestive enzymes.

**plasma:** the liquid part of blood

**prediabetes:** borderline high blood sugar levels, which indicate an increased risk of developing diabetes

**retinopathy:** damage to small blood vessels in the back of the eye (retina) that causes blurred vision and other vision problems

**simple carbohydrates:** carbohydrates that come from sugars, such as table sugar, processed flour, candy, soda, and snack foods

**stem cells:** primary cells that can become any type of cell. Researchers are investigating use of stem cells to replace damaged beta cells in the pancreas.

**type 1 diabetes:** a disease, most often diagnosed in children and young adults, in which the body produces little or no insulin

**type 2 diabetes:** the most common form of diabetes in which the body either does not produce enough insulin or does not use insulin properly. Type 2 typically affects middle-aged and older people, but younger adults and children can get it too.

**visualization:** technique to reduce stress and pain by picturing a healthy body or relaxed setting

**yoga:** body-mind relaxation that combines deep breathing with physical poses.

# RESOURCES

## BOOKS

Barrier, Phyllis. *Type 2 Diabetes for Beginners*. Alexandria, VA: American Diabetes Association, 2005.

Edelman, Steven V. *Taking Control of Your Diabetes*. 3rd ed. Caddo, OK: Professional Communications, 2007.

Ezrin, Calvin. *The Type 2 Diabetes Diet Book*. 3rd ed. Lincolnwood, IL: NTC/Contemporary, 1999.

Gray, Shirley Wimbish. *Living with Diabetes*. Chanhassen, MN: Child's World, 2003.

U.S. Department of Health and Human Services. *Keep the Beat: Heart Healthy Recipes*. National Institutes of Health, National Heart, Lung, and Blood Institute, NIH Publication No. 03-2921, 2003.

Webb, Robyn. *Diabetic Meals in 30 Minutes—Or Less!* Alexandria, VA: American Diabetes Association, 1996.

## ORGANIZATIONS

American Diabetes Association
1701 North Beauregard Street
Alexandria, VA 22311
(800) DIABETES (342-2383)
askada@diabetes.org
www.diabetes.org
This national organization offers online and printed information about diabetes, local programs and resources, such as finding diabetes educators, and an online questionnaire that calculates an individual's risk of acquiring diabetes.

Diabetes Exercise and Sports Association
8001 Montcastle Drive
Nashville, TN 37221
(800) 898-4322
http://www.diabetes-exercise.org
This national organization, with local chapters and a newsletter, connects people with diabetes who enjoy healthy and safe exercise.

Disability Rights Education and Defense Fund
2213 Sixth Street
Berkeley, CA 94710
(510) 644-2555
http://www.dredf.org
This law center project advocates for people with disabilities and health issues in schools and workplaces.

Juvenile Diabetes Research Foundation International
120 Wall Street
New York, NY 10005-4001
(800) 533-2873
info@jdrf.org
http://www.jdrf.org
This international organization focuses on type 1 diabetes and raises funds, sponsors clinical research trials, runs diabetes camps, and publishes *Teen Countdown* magazine and *Kids Online* and *Life with Diabetes* e-newsletters.

MedicAlert Foundation International
2323 Colorado Avenue
Turlock, CA 95383
(888) 633-4298
http://www.medicalert.org
This organization sells MedicAlert® bracelets and necklaces for people with diabetes or other serious illnesses. It also runs an emergency response center and notifies family members in case of emergency.

National Diabetes Education Program
1 Diabetes Way
Bethesda, MD 20892-3600
(800) 438-5383
http://www.ndep.nih.gov
This general information site offers online brochures and access to current diabetes studies.

National Diabetes Information Clearinghouse
1 Information Way
Bethesda, MD 20892-3560
(800) 860-8747
http://diabetes.niddk.nih.gov/
This site, part of the U.S. government's National Institute of Diabetes and Digestive and Kidney Diseases, offers downloadable and printed brochures on a range of topics affecting people with diabetes.

National Information Center for Children and Youth with Disabilities (NICHY)
P.O. Box 1492
Washington, DC 20013
(800) 695-0285
http://www.nichy.org
http://www.kidsource.com
This public agency provides information and referrals.

National Institute of Diabetes and Digestive and Kidney Diseases
Building 31, Room 9A04
Center Drive, MSC 2560
Bethesda, MD 20892-2560
http://www.niddk.nih.gov
This government organization conducts clinical research into diabetes and related illnesses.

TCOYD—Taking Control of Your Diabetes
1110 Camino Del Mar, Suite B
Del Mar, CA 92014
(800)99-TCOYD (998-2693)
http://www.tcoyd.org
This organization produces conferences and health fairs for people with diabetes and their families, dynamic newsletters, and an excellent website.

## WEBSITES

*The ADA Wizdom Youth Zone*
http://www.diabetes.org/wizdom
The American Diabetes Association (ADA) site offers fun information kits for kids.

*American Dietetic Association*
http://www.eatright.org
The American Dietetic Association is the world's largest organization devoted to food and nutrition, offering meal planning information for people with diabetes.

*Children with Diabetes*
http://www.childrenwithdiabetes.com
This site offers resources and chat rooms for kids with diabetes and their families.

*Diabetes Camping Association*
http://www.diabetescamp.org
This agency focuses on camps for children with diabetes.

*National Institutes of Health National Center for Complementary and Alternative Medicine*
http://nccam.nih.gov
Read results from studies that investigate alternative treatments for diabetes.

*Reality Check*
http://www.reality check.org
This Australian-based site is for young adults with diabetes.

*We Can!* (Ways to Enhance Children's Activity and Nutrition)
http://www.nhlbi.nih.gov/health/public/heart/obesity/wecan/
Find practical tools from four National Institutes of Health for parents and caregivers who want to help their preteens with weight control.

# SOURCES

8 Chris Feudtner, *Bittersweet: Diabetes, Insulin, and the Transformation of Illness* (Chapel Hill: University of North Carolina Press, 2003), 4.
8 Ibid., 4, 224.
8 Ibid., 5.
13 Jared, personal interview with author, Chicago, IL, June 16, 2006.
16 Reuters, "Diabetes Rate Doubled in Last 30 Years, http://www.CNN.com. (June 22, 2006)
17 Carl, personal interview with author, Noblesville, IN, June 15, 2006.
27 Marc Santora, "East Meets West, Adding Pounds and Peril," *The New York Times*, January 12, 2006, 1A.
34 Jared, personal interview.
35 Christine Potema, ed., *JDRF Illinois News*, Fall 2006, 6.
38 Ann, personal interview with author, Evanston, IL, June 13, 2006.
45 Emily, personal interview with author, Chicago, IL, May 30, 2006.
51 Jared, personal interview.
52 Richard Bernstein, *Dr. Bernstein's Diabetes Solution: The Complete Guide to Achieving Normal Blood Sugars* (Boston: Little, Brown and Co., 2003), 205.
54 Bob, personal interview with author, Wilmette, IL, June 28, 2006.
56 Emily, personal interview.
57 Ibid.
58 Alex Berenson, "A Ray of Hope for Diabetics," *New York Times*, March 2, 2006, C4.
61 Jared, personal interview.
66 Emily, personal interview.
67 Jared, personal interview.
68 Ibid.
72 Rebecca Lanning, ed., *American Diabetes Association Complete Guide to Diabetes*, 4th ed. (Alexandria, VA: American Diabetes Association, 2005) 311.

78 Melissa, personal interview with author, Northbrook, IL July 11, 2006.
79 Ann, personal interview.
80 Ibid.
80 Melissa, personal interview.
83 Emily, personal interview.
83 Carl, personal interview.
84 Tracey Koepke, "Stress Management as a Factor in Healthy Living," *DukeMedNews*, January 18, 2002, http://www.dukemednews.org/av/medminute.php?id-5268. (June 20, 2007)
85 Jared, personal interview.
92 Canadian Diabetes Association, "The History of Diabetes," 2007, http://www.diabetes.ca/section_About/timeline.asp. (June 20, 2007)
95 Melissa, personal interview.
98 Paula Ford-Martin, *The Everything Diabetes Book* (Avon, MA: Adams Media, 2004), 290.
99 Jared, personal interview.

# Selected Bibliography

Bernstein, Richard. *Dr. Bernstein's Diabetes Solution: The Complete Guide to Achieving Normal Blood Sugars*. Boston: Little, Brown and Co., 2003. 30.

Center for Nutrition Policy and Promotion. "How Much Are You Eating?" United States Department of Agriculture, 2002.

Centers for Disease Control and Prevention, National Health and Nutrition Examination Survey. *National Diabetes Fact Sheet*, 2005. Atlanta, GA: U.S. Department of Health and Human Services, 2005.

Collazo-Clavell, Maria, ed. *Mayo Clinic on Managing Diabetes*. Rochester, MN: Mayo Clinic, 2001.

Dragisic, Patricia, ed. *The American Medical Association Complete Medical Encyclopedia*. New York: Random House, 2003.

Feudtner, Chris. *Bittersweet: Diabetes, Insulin, and the Transformation of Illness*. Chapel Hill: University of North Carolina Press, 2003.

Ford-Martin, Paula. *The Everything Diabetes Book*. Avon, MA: Adams Media, 2004.

Gehling, Eve. *The Family & Friends' Guide to Diabetes*. New York: John Wiley & Sons, 2000.

Grady, Denise. "Link between Diabetes and Alzheimer's Disease." *New York Times*, July 17, 2006, A15.

Guthrie, Diana. *The Diabetes Sourcebook*. New York: McGraw-Hill, 2004.

JDRF. "Diabetes Complications." *Juvenile Diabetes Research Foundation International*, December 15, 2006. http://www.jdrf.org/index.cfm?page_id=101308. (June 21, 2007)

Lanning, Rebecca, ed. *American Diabetes Association Complete Guide to Diabetes*. 4th ed. Alexandria, VA: American Diabetes Association, 2005.

LifeMed Media, "Blood Glucose Monitoring." *dLife*. August 29, 2006. http://www.dlife.com/dLife/do/ShowContent/blood_sugar_management/testing/. (June 21, 2007)

National Diabetes Information Clearinghouse. *Diabetes Overview*. U. S. Department of Health and Human Services. NIH Publication 06-3875, April 2006.

Rosenthal, Elisabeth. "Drug Can Prevent Diabetes in Many at High Risk Study Suggests." *International Herald Tribune*. September 17, 2006. http://www.nytimes.com/2006/09/17/world/17diabetes.html. (June 20, 2007)

Santora, Marc. "Concern Grows over Increase in Diabetes around World." *New York Times*, June 11, 2006.

"WHO: Welcome to the Diabetes Programme," *The World Health Organization*, 2007. http://www.who.int/diabetes/en. (June 20, 2007)

Woolston, Chris. "Type 2 Diabetes: Growing Epidemic Among Teens." *Consumer Health Interactive*. 2001. http://www.healthresources.caremark.com/topic/type2 kids. (June 20, 2007)

# INDEX

acupunture, 89
African Americans, 21, 27
age, 28
alcohol, 50
alpha-glucosidase inhibitors, 58
Alzheimer's disease, 73
American Diabetes Association (ADA), 17, 36, 41, 46, 54, 86; recommendations of, 52, 85
amyloid, 73
animal testing, 92–93
antibodies, 20, 21, 56, 97–98
A1C test, 32
Aretaeus, 8
Asians, 21, 27
autoantibodies, 21
autoimmune disease, 21

Banting, Frederick, 93, 94
Best, Charles, 93, 94
beta cells, 10, 11, 20, 21, 90, 95, 97, 98
biguanides, 58
biofeedback, 89
blindness, 70
blood glucose, 30
bloodletting, 91
blood pressure, 55, 69, 72, 87, 88
blood samples, measuring, 53–54
blood sugar (glucose), 8, 10, 13, 14, 15, 51
blood sugar levels, 13, 30, 41; alcohol and, 50; controlling, 98; factors affecting, 65; medicines for stabilizing, 57–58; recording, 55; testing, 30–32, 52, 53–55, 61
blood sugar meters, 34, 37, 38, 52, 53, 54, 62, 86, 98
blood vessel disease, 69
Brantley, Jeffrey, 84

calories, 44
camps, diabetes, 78
carb counting, 41–42
carbohydrates, 40–42, 44
cardiovascular disease, 69
care team, 33–36
case histories: Abby, 64–65; Brianna, 75–76; Carl, 83; Emily, 45, 56–57, 66, 83; Jamie, 90–91; Jared, 7, 13, 38, 51, 61, 67–68, 99; Jay, 19; Jim, 37; Melissa, 78, 80, 94–95; Sam, 29–30; Shawna, 18–19, 35
Centers for Disease Control and Prevention (CDC), 16, 20
chi, 89
children, 20, 63, 78–81, 90
chromosomes, 25
Collip, J. B., 93, 94
comic books, 82
continuous glucose monitor (CGM), 53, 63
cure, 17, 95–98: research for a cure, 91–94

dehydration, 64, 67, 91
depression, 76–77
diabetes: causes and risk factors of, 19, 21, 22, 25–28, 32, 33; complications of, 16, 30,

38, 65–73, 94, 98; control and prevention of, 17, 23, 33, 51–52, 74, 81; cure, 17, 95–97; learning about, 17, 33, 34, 98; living with, 36, 45, 57, 67, 72, 74, 76, 98–99; mellitus, 9; names of, 8, 9, 16; symptoms of, 22, 68; testing for, 30–33; treatment of, 22, 23, 33, 38, 51–52, 53, 57, 95–98
diabetes, types of, 19–24; gestational, 23–24; maturity-onset diabetes of the young (MODY), 24; type 1, 18, 19–21, 22, 25, 58, 68, 70, 95, 97; type 2, 19, 20, 21–23, 25, 58, 68, 70, 73, 84
diabetes educators, 34
diabetic ketoacidosis (DKA), 67–69
diabetics. *See* people with diabetes
diagnostic tests: fasting plasma glucose test, 30–31; glycosylated hemoglobin (A1C) test, 32; oral glucose tolerance test, 32; random plasma glucose test, 31–32
diaries, 45, 54, 55
diet, 17, 20, 27, 37, 38–50, 72
dietician, 34–35
digestion, 10
digestive organs, 12
discrimination, 79
DNA, 95. *See also* genes
Dobson, Matthew, 8–9
doctors, 33–34, 35–36
dogs, contributions to research by, 92, 93

education, 17, 33, 34
emergency management, 65, 66, 67, 85–86
emotions, 76–78, 81, 83–85
endocrine system, 10
endocrinologist, 34
epidemic proportions, diabetes reaching, 15–16
ethnic background, 21, 27
exercise, 17, 20, 23, 28, 33, 51–52, 85, 88. *See also* walking
eye health, 15, 35–36, 70–71

family history, 25, 27
fasting plasma glucose test, 30–31
fats in foods, 42, 44
fiber, 41
food exchanges, 47
food labels, 43, 48–49
food management, 38–50, 86. *See also* diet
foot care, 36, 73–74
friends and family, 77, 86
Froguel, Phillipe, 96
future, 95–99

gender, 27
genes, 25, 95–97
gestational diabetes, 23–24
glucagon, 65
glucose. *See* blood sugar (glucose)
glucose impairment, 33
glucose meter. *See* blood sugar meter
glucose tolerance test, 32
glycosylated hemoglobin (A1C) test, 32
glycogen, 13, 51, 65

healthy lifestyle, 17, 23, 33, 51
heart disease, 69
high blood sugar, 30, 66, 67
Hispanics, 21, 27

**115**

history, 8–9, 91–95
honeymoon phase, 60, 97
hormones, 10, 81, 84; in pregnancy, 23, 24
Human Genome Project, 95
hyperglycemia, 30, 66, 67
hypoglycemia, 30, 50, 65, 66–67

identification bracelets and necklaces, 66
immune system, 20, 21
immune therapy, 97–98
implanted monitors, 98
incretin mimetics, 58
infections, 15, 20, 54, 70, 73–74
insulin, 8, 10, 13, 20, 58–63; discovery of, 92–94; types of, 59–60
insulin delivery methods: inhalers, 63; jet injectors, 61, 62; pens, 61–62; pumps, 62–63; syringes, 61
insulin reaction (hypoglycemia), 66–67
insulin resistance, 22, 81, 84
interstitial fluid, 53
islets of Langerhans, 10, 11, 92, 97

ketoacidosis, 66, 67–68
ketones, 68
kidney disease (nephropathy), 71–72
kidneys, 9, 13, 58, 71

lancet, 53
Langerhans, Paul, 92
liver, 10, 11, 13, 58
logs and diaries, 45, 54, 55
low blood suagr, 30, 50, 65, 66–67

Macleod, John, 93, 94

maturity-onset diabetes of the young (MODY), 24
meal plans, 45–46, 55. *See also* diet; food management
medical alert bracelets and necklaces, 66
medication, 57–58, 98; antirejection, 97. *See also* insulin
meditation, 88
memory loss, 73
metabolism, 10
meters. *See* blood sugar meters
Minkowski, Oskar, 92
monitors. *See* blood sugar monitors
Morrison, Adam, 26

National Institute of Diabetes and Digestive and Kidney Diseases, 33
Native Americans, 27
needles, 59, 61, 83
nephropathy, 71–72
nerve damage, 69–70
neuropathy, 70
newsmakers with diabetes, 26
Nobel Prize, 94
nutrition labels, 43, 48–49

obesity, 20, 23, 27. *See also* weight
*Omega Boy versus Doctor Diabetes*, 82
oral glucose tolerance test, 32

pancreas, 11, 20, 21; medication and insulin and, 57–59, 97–98; in pregnancy, 23; transplants, 97
parents, 78–79, 80, 81, 83
Peninsula Medical School (UK), 90

people with diabetes, 16; ages of, 19–20, 22; children, 20, 63, 78–81; famous, 26; numbers of, 15–16, 33; support for, 77; teens, 81–83
physical activity. *See* exercise
placenta, 23
plan making, 85–86. *See also* meal plans
portion sizes, 45, 46
prediabetes, 16, 32–33
pregnancy, 23
prevention, 17, 23, 33, 51, 74, 81
proteins, 42, 44

random plasma glucose test, 31–32
"rate your plate," 46
record keeping, 45, 54, 55
relaxation techniques, 86–89
research for a cure. *See* cure
retinopathy, 70, 71
risk factors, 25, 26–29
Rossini, Aldo, 16

salt intake, 72
school, 79–81
skin care, 36, 73
smoking, 74, 81
stem cells, 96
stress management, 83–85
stroke, 69
sulfonylureas, 57, 91
symptoms: blurred vision, 15; fatigue, 14; headaches, 15; healing difficulties, 15; hunger, increased, 14; thirst, excessive, 8, 9, 13; urination, excessive, 8, 13; weight changes, 14
support groups, 38, 76, 86

teenagers, 81–83
tooth and mouth care, 36, 73
transplants, 97
treatments, 22, 23, 33, 38, 51–52, 53, 57, 95–98
type 1 diabetes, 18, 19–21, 22, 25, 58, 68, 70, 95, 97
type 2 diabetes, 19, 20, 21–23, 25, 58, 68, 70, 73, 84

urine tests, 7, 8–9, 68, 72

vegan diet, 50
vision problems, 15. *See also* retinopathy
visualization, 87
Von Mering, Joseph, 92

walking, 33, 37
Washington, Kamaal, 82
Washington, Malcolm, 82
weight, 22, 27–28, 34, 58; unexplained changes in, 14
Willis, Thomas, 8, 9
World Health Organization, 15

yoga, 51, 88

# About the Author

Marlene Targ Brill is an award-winning author of sixty-five books. Her book *Tourette Syndrome* for this series was named a Bank Street College Best Children's Book of the Year. Marlene especially likes to write about ways to help readers feel better and understand how their bodies function. As a young student, Marlene enjoyed learning about the body and wanted to work in medicine. Instead, she became a teacher of children with special needs. Now she writes about a variety of topics, especially in the health care field, on topics such as Alzheimer's disease, Down syndrome, and autism.

# Photo Acknowledgments

The images in this book are used with the permission of: © Todd Strand/Independent Picture Service, pp. 3, 7, 18, 29, 37, 43, 52, 54, 56, 59, 61, 62, 64, 75, 85, 90; Library of Congress (LC-USZ62-117971), p. 9; © Laura Westlund/Independent Picture Service, pp. 11, 12; PhotoDisc Royalty Free by Getty Images, pp. 14, 40, 47, 51, 87, 88; © Jeff Greenberg/Alamy, p. 17; © age fotostock/SuperStock, pp. 24, 35; © Elsa/Getty Images, p. 26; © Tim Boyle/Getty Images, p. 31; © Royalty-Free/CORBIS, pp. 36, 39; Copyright © 2007 American Diabetes Association from http://www.diabetes.org Reprinted with permission from The American Diabetes Association, p. 46; Comstock Images, pp. 49, 95; © Deborah C. Mink, p. 55; Courtesy Medtronic, Inc., p. 63; © SIU/Visuals Unlimited, p. 71; © Patrice Beriault/Peter Arnold, Inc., p. 72; Photo provided by Omega 7 Inc., p. 82; © Jessica Rinaldi/Getty Images, p. 83; © Christian Hoehn/Stone/Getty Images, p. 84; © Bettmann/CORBIS, pp. 91, 93; © Philippe Huguen/AFP/Getty Images, p. 96.

Front cover: © PHOTOTAKE Inc./Alamy (left); © Todd Strand/Independent Picture Service (right).

Mt. Sterling Public Library
60 W. Columbus St.
Mt. Sterling, Ohio 43143